The Cowboy's
Rebellious Bride

The Cowboy's Rebellious Bride

A McCall Brothers Romance

Laurie LeClair

TULE
PUBLISHING

Dedication

To my beloved husband, Jim LeClair. Thank you for "going journeying" with me on this great, big adventure of life and dreams! Love you with all my heart.

Chapter One

"WHAT THE HEY? Did someone die and no one told me?" Cody McCall strolled in to The Giddy Up, his recently polished boots softly scraping over the well-worn threshold.

He tipped his tan cowboy hat back and frowned at the low murmurs of the thin Friday night crowd. With their heads hung and the air flat, Cody wondered if he'd stumbled in to a funeral home instead of his favorite bar.

The last thing he'd expected at prime time was a bunch of sad sacks. "Seriously?"

His oldest brother Caleb and youngest brother Conner had forced him to come to town and shake off the dust of his nearly ten days working the cattle and land at their family's ranch.

Not a whole lot of shaking going on here.

They'd stayed behind at the house to play cards with their widowed Gramps—his brothers' Friday night ritual with their grandfather and some of his old cronies and longtime neighbors.

Gramps was their top priority. Nothing else mattered to

the McCall brothers. *Not one damn thing!*

Keeping Gramps well and cared for proved tricky when he hardly ate. The shock at seeing him drop a few more pounds this time away still rocked Cody.

Of course, the same question rushed back to him time and time again. What could he do to get his beloved Gramps to want to really live again? He'd give everything just to see the best man he ever knew to be happy, to see that genuine smile come easy and stay.

Cody had to find that one thing.

He'd been hard pressed to leave Gramps at the McCall ranch forty minutes ago. Cody found his grandfather firmly in the clutches of grieving for his late grandmother. Eight months still wasn't long enough to dull the edges of that pain. Maybe nothing would after fifty years of wedded bliss.

Piled on top, suspended in disbelief, there hung the stunning knowledge that he'd heavily mortgaged the ranch to pay the hefty medical bills from Grams' illness and expensive treatments.

The latest notice from the bank sat in bold black letters against the stark white paper in the center of Gramps' oak desk. Staring at it made everything more real and urgent. Cody's mind blared with the shocking tidbit. *Time was running out for the McCall family...*

"First up on the agenda: save the ranch." *It would kill Gramps if he lost his home, too.*

He blew out a pent-up breath, forcing the fresh, gripping

waves of mourning to ease from behind his ribs. It barely shifted.

Looking around the interior of the bar now—the walls lined with posters of country music legends, the pool table stood empty and silent, and the dust motes floating in the dim lights from the antler chandeliers—he shook his head in disgust.

"And I thought I was coming for a good time, too."

The rustic bar—the wood weathered to a warm, honey color—spanned nearly the width of the long room with a few of the stools occupied. The cowboys there glanced over their shoulders and then turned back again, like bobble heads on a stick.

It wasn't much better at the tables lining the smooth, worn dance space. He recognized every one of the nearly dozen people here. Who wouldn't in the small ranch community?

His cursory look took in his cousin with his white cowboy hat pitched down to cover his eyes and a former high school friend at one table, sprawled in chairs with their legs stretched out. If they sank any lower, they'd slide right out of their chairs and under the dang table.

And on the other side, the three hometown girls were huddled off to his right, tucked in a corner. They whispered like a bunch of buzzing bees now.

Where was the band? The tiny platform, littered with discarded instruments, stood empty and silent. *Don't tell me there's no music, too!*

Never mind that. Where was his best friend, his cohort in all things fun and outrageous? A pang shot through him.

He hadn't come back from working long, back-breaking days at the McCall ranch only to be met with listlessness. Cody needed to keep his bottled-up emotions from burning a hole clear through him, like a powerful fireball shot through his middle and leaving flames behind. He'd kept a lid on his wild side far too long already.

"Oh, hell no!" Cody whistled between his lips. The others jarred, straightening their spines and taking notice. "Wake up, people! Cods is in town and we've got a party to start."

Finally, his cousin, Jacob, shoved back his hat, jumped to his feet, and then rushed to greet him. Reaching out, he shook Cody's hand and slapped him on the back. "Hey, about time you got here and livened things up."

"You think? What, do I have to do everything around here? Can't you lug heads do anything without me?" He grinned.

"Thought you'd never get back, cuz." A wistfulness edged his words.

"Yeah, it's been too long."

"How's Uncle Left doing?" A shadow crossed his young, expressive features. As a Laramie, he favored his father's side—dark hair and blue eyes. But he had his momma's tender heart.

The knot tightened in Cody's gut. "Worse. He could use some of Aunt Sissy's award-winning fried chicken."

"Coming right up. Mom loves spoiling her big brother."

Cody greeted more of his friends with a handshake or a fist bump. "How's it going? Good to see you."

"Not the same without you, bud." Sterling Tucker clapped him on the shoulder. "Got some serious drinking to do." His high school buddy, known for slugging back a few too many, grinned from ear-to-ear. Not much changed in the last eight years since graduation for good ol' Tuck—work the range and party harder. Throw in a few pretty girls now and then and the man stayed happy.

A sliver of awareness snaked through Cody. Maybe he wasn't that much different than his friend. He brushed that bothersome thought away. *Too many truths were surfacing since Grams passed.*

He stood in the midst of his cousin and friends, catching up on the rodeo circuit, the bucking broncs he used to ride, and the upcoming season.

"Pop's setting up a training center, Cody." Tuck nodded his head. "You know, these young guns need some help learning the ropes. I'm up for steer wrestling. Got a spot open. You interested in teaching bareback bronc riding?"

"Me?" A part of Cody itched to get back in the ring. Leaving the circuit last year to come home due to Grams' declining health hadn't fazed him. He'd walked away for his family. *No regrets!*

However, staying away after she passed, his sponsors dropping him, and hurting for cash to give to Gramps reminded him he wished he could slip back in that life. That and loving what he did—the horses, the challenge, the rush.

But his history, first watching his parents and then Grams leave, proved he didn't want to lose any more of the people he loved than he already had. *Can't walk away from Gramps or my family.*

"He wants you. The best. Good pay, too. Come on, what do you say?" Tuck rubbed his hands together. "Aren't you just dying to get back on one of those broncs?"

Sterling Sr. mentored *him* as a kid. *Good man.* "You had me at I'm the best and good pay."

He chuckled and his cousin and friends joined in.

"Hey, Cody. You ready to dance?" Sandy Owens slid up beside him and nudged his arm. The pretty brunette batted her eyelashes at him.

Turning, he found the girls eyeing him and his friends. They were younger, gussied up in brand spanking new duds—two dressed in Daisy Dukes, tight shirts, and pastel-colored cowgirl hats firmly in place. He glanced down at Sandy's bright, orange-flamed boots. "Whoa, girl! You're gonna burn up the floor with those beauts."

"Don't you know it, Cody McCall. And I'm giving you first dibs on helping me break them in."

His cousin and friends ribbed him. "Go for it, Cods!"

Cody scratched his clean-shaven jaw, wondering if her

offer held more than he'd willingly seek. Dancing and having a good time seemed all he could muster tonight. Flashy, needy girls weren't his type. Heck, *relationships* weren't his type. With Gramps and Gram setting the bar high, not just any girl would do. "Don't think I got the fire extinguisher handy."

"I got it for you, girl!" Tucker hooted, making her smile and look him up and down.

The rest of them chuckled at the pair's eagerness now.

A shrill whistle rent the air. His heart jumped. Cody knew that sound. He taught her that.

Grinning, he jerked around. He found her easily coming up behind the waiting group of cowgirls. *Beautiful.* Blonde—she'd cut her hair to shoulder-length and added a sweep of bangs—and with big, brown eyes staring him down, she was the best thing he'd seen in weeks. She barely reached five-foot-two, standing with her hands planted on her hips and tapping the toe of her pretty pink boot.

"About time you got here, Cods!" Hannah Prescott laughed, well, more like shrieked, and then launched herself at him.

Cody caught her up in his arms, holding her off the ground and to his chest. Tiny and petite, she fit perfectly. It felt far too good to hug his best friend again after weeks of missing her. And she smelled like sunshine, warm, fresh and breezy, and home.

Longing and nostalgia coupled and sucker punched him

square in the chest. He shook those strange feelings off and focused on the moment and getting back to an even footing. "Dang, girl! Did you shrink while I was gone?"

"Funny, McCall." She pressed her face to his cheek. "Missed you, cowboy." She squeezed him around his neck one last time before he set her down. Then she jabbed him in the gut. It packed about a tenth of her power and strength.

"Is that all you got? You're getting weak." He laughed at the flash of mutiny in her eyes. Cody loved pushing her buttons.

"Just for that you're buying me a drink." She grabbed his arm and steered him away from the others.

"Not even a howdy do first?" But he went along as the guys and girls called them back. She directed him to a stool near the end of the long bar.

"Come on, Hannah. Don't keep him all for yourself." Jacob tried to intervene. "The band will be back any minute and you're stealing the life of the party away?"

"Simmer down. I'll send him along before it gets dark out." Her sass met with more joking from the guys, but they had come to life and began to flirt with the girls nearby.

"What'll you have?" He spotted Buzz hauling in two cases of beer.

"Whiskey, Buzz." Hannah leaned across the wood surface to get the bartender's attention when he dipped his head, the bottles clinking as he filled up the cooler.

"Be right there." He nodded.

"We celebrating?" Something clamped around Cody's windpipe. He coughed to clear it. "Did he ask you yet?"

"Rodney Ellis, you mean? That man…" She plopped down on the seat, her hair swinging across her lips. She hooked the piece behind her cute little ear. "Wait a minute. You knew?"

"I saw him before I headed out and you were—where, again? On the road, somewhere. He's got the fever. You know, the one where he turns all red and blotchy when he even thinks about popping the question."

"Ah, are you talking about yourself here?" She made a noise in the back of her throat. Angled toward him, she crossed her jean clad legs, swinging her bright pink cowgirl boot. "Where were you when I needed you to talk about this last week? You could at least pick up or text me back."

"What am I supposed to do with a cell out on the range? Climb to the top of the ridge and stick my arm to the north and my leg to the east to try to get reception." He chuckled.

She folded her arms over her chest and stared him down.

Cody gulped hard. He'd been that guy—the fever fella. He suspected Grams getting sick and her last wish to see all her grandsons married had something to do with it. He'd gotten within a hairsbreadth of proposing to Tabitha a year ago. Thank God he'd changed his mind—or someone else had helped rub the dust off his eyes—in the nick of time. *Wake up call! Thank you, Jesus!*

"I'm waiting."

"Yep, life of the party Cody. That's me. Why mess with a good thing?" But it stung to recall how close he'd gotten to ruining his entire life. What a fool he'd been to think she'd want the same things he did! *The ranch, ha!* She'd rented a high-priced apartment in Austin and planned on moving there the moment the I-dos were a done deal.

"Escape artist. How did you do it? Tell me, so I can, too."

"Shots." Buzz, tall and thin and about as weathered as the bar looked, plunked down the glasses and poured. Once done, he gave them a jaunty salute. "Holler when you want some more, y'all."

Hannah nudged Cody. "Advice. Fast." She picked up her drink when he did.

"He's a decent guy." He shrugged. *Safe. Boring.*

The pale tenderfoot didn't seem up to her usual tough cowboy standards. He couldn't picture Hannah settling for him. His chest tightened at the thought of her with Rodney or anyone, for that matter. *Whoa! Where did that come from?*

"I don't want to hurt his feelings." She grimaced. "Or lose his daddy's business. He wants to team up with me and be a stock contractor. Him?"

"Timid. Tame for you." The words tumbled out of him, fast and blunt.

"Exactly. Not my type."

"Why'd you date him, anyway? His bankroll?" That was not like his Hannah.

"Skip it. Next question, Cods."

"Escape plan, anyone?" He lifted his glass and they bolted back the whiskey at the same time. His lips tingled and the burn slid down until it hit his belly. The instant warmth spread through his body.

"Whoo!" She slammed down the shot glass. "You, my friend, need to tell him for me."

"Huh? Why me?"

"Because you owe me, big time for saving your butt."

He scowled. "How so?"

"Ah, like, every time a woman comes around. They think since we're such good friends there's a thing going on."

"I figure that works both ways, Hannah Banana." He grinned when she grimaced at his nickname for her.

"So, use it this time. Good ol' Rodney is clueless."

A commotion from the platform caught their attention as the three-man band came back in, grabbed up their instruments, and then hunkered down. Gunther tapped the keys of the old, upright piano, Jackson—another cousin and Jacob's brother—adjusted the mic. Harv softly tapped the bow on the fiddle.

Hannah plucked off Cody's cowboy hat and then settled it on her head. Next, she reached over and ruffled his hair. "Show us your moves, Cods!"

She hopped off the bar stool, clutched his hand, and then walked backward, dragging him to the dance floor.

Jackson strummed his guitar. The first few chords of the

familiar, rowdy tune cut through the stale air.

"Now, we're talking." Cody grinned as their friends joined Hannah and him. "That's right! Low places…"

They sang along, dancing and hooting and hollering. He swung a laughing Hannah around and nearly bumped into Tuck and Sandy. Cody tugged Hannah a little closer, protecting her from poking elbows and stomping boots.

Looking up, way up, at him, she captured his stare. Her tender smile spread slow and wide and her brown eyes sparkled, melting him. His breath hitched. A steady buzz hummed in his blood.

It was the whiskey, right?

Tell me, it's just the whiskey whooshing through my veins and nothing else!

Chapter Two

Hannah Prescott waved off Cody for the next dance. Four in a row was plenty for the moment. "I need a beer or a dozen." She grabbed the two long necks Buzz plunked down on the bar. "You are my new bestie, Buzz." She turned to hand a bottle to her friend.

But Cody was off again, dancing with Julie Garcia, who had eyes for every boy in town. Listening to her go on and on about the merits of every single guy under thirty in Honor, Texas earlier forced Hannah to hightail it to the ladies' room and hide for a good ten minutes. *Not easy when you don't have to go and hadn't brought your cell with you.* The girl just wanted to marry a cowboy, settle down, and pop out little cow patties.

Not my thing! Loving someone meant getting hurt.

"Good luck with Cods, Jules." Her murmured words were low and soon swallowed up in the bottle she tipped back, chugging it down. The cold, strong ale hit the spot, washing away the heat flooding her body. She slapped down the empty one on the bar and started on the next one, sipping this time.

Learning back with her elbows on the worn, round edge of the bar, she watched her best friend as more than one of her girlfriends joined in the dance, this time swinging him around. His suede hat, still on her head, held his scent. Her breath hitched as the hint of musk and man combined to drift over her.

His dark blond hair, longer and lightened by the long days in the sun, had felt so good through her fingers earlier.

She gulped hard.

Being around stammering Rodney had certainly made her appreciate a manly man more. But the greenhorn was a good guy, true and honest. He loved her, or so he thought. *Yeah, just wait, he'd change his tune soon. Like most every guy she'd ever known did.*

However, she did not love Rodney. *Never could. Never would.* Because, now watching Cody—throwing his head back and laughing—from a distance, Hannah Prescott's heart tugged, hard and sharp. Finally, she admitted what she'd been hiding from herself for far too long. How could she *not* love her best friend, Cody McCall?

The truth slammed into her like one of the thousand pound bulls she raised for the rodeos. Her heart jerked and quivered again, stuttering to a halt.

"No!" *Please, no! Not that!*

Loving someone left you broken and hurt. Just ask her dear, late mother how it ruined her entire life being cheated on by Hannah's daddy.

He'd hid it well for years while Hannah was growing up, but some clues could not be ignored. Up until she was eight, her life had been idyllic. Then just like that, everything crashed around her—needing a confidante, her mother had blurted out the ugly truth. The pieces fell into place, making complete and utter sense.

The blinders came off that day. The innocent little girl disappeared in one swift, searing flash of pain. In her eyes, he was flawed beyond repair. Even his charm couldn't disguise his selfishness any longer. *Her daddy wasn't the man she'd thought he was.*

The haunting memories of her mother pleading with him to end it rattled through Hannah now. The sobs grew louder in her mind.

Biting down hard on the inside of her cheek forced her back to the here and now and away from those aching images, the sounds of doors slamming echoing, and the sharp taste of bitterness. Finally, the past faded away.

Phew! Never, ever going back to that chaos! She'd be damned if history repeated itself with her.

Hannah didn't have time for feelings or wayward emotions, never mind the *L* word. *It felt awful! Like some kind of disease or addiction!*

"Stubborn animals, and burning alcohol, not necessarily in that order, are so much easier to deal with than people," she whispered under her breath.

She ran a stock contractor business, one of the few women who did in a man's world of raising bulls. She'd more than earned her fair, yet tough, reputation among them. Seven long years gave her the hard work, dedication, and the experience she needed to take the next giant step—getting one of her bulls to the ultimate show.

All she wanted was that big break, the one where one of her prized bulls made it to the PRCA finals in December in Vegas and outlasted the best rodeo cowboy in the business. It was so close, she could practically taste it.

She wasn't about to let Rodney—someone who had cash and no grit or respect from her peers—to swoop in and take over. Hannah earned the right to play with the big boys. No way would she succumb to the lure of endless capital to buy her way to the top faster. What price would she have to pay then?

Your dignity, girl!

Nope. No way, Jose. It cost too much.

But Cody? It couldn't be! The second he figured it out, he'd drop her. She'd seen it countless times before. He did not do permanent.

Neither do you, girl! The pain and suffering over a man just wasn't worth the trouble.

They'd joke about how the girls swooned around Cody. He'd cringe at the obvious interest, especially the clingy, overzealous ones. Slowly, without them even being aware, he'd ease away, putting distance and then, before they even knew what happened, he was gone.

"YO, HANNAH," CODY called to her, gaining her full attention. His smile flashed across his rugged, square face. "Dance with me."

Her chest squeezed at his endearing grin. Oh, and those light green eyes of his didn't disappoint, either. And the adorable small dimple in his chin…

"Beer first, Cods!" She held up the brown bottle. "Lots of it, too." *About a case or two to drown in.*

"Chug a lug and then shake a leg, girl!" He found Sandy at his side, more than willing to take her place.

Sandy gave her a wave and raised and lowered her eyebrows. Her girlfriend giggled as Cody guided her back to the dance floor.

A stab of envy at how easily he moved along poked her. It had always been there. But somehow this time, coming back together after weeks of her traveling and him working the ranch, she felt it sharper and it left a bitter taste behind.

Not the green-eyed monster!

Is this how her mother had felt?

Being away from him on the tour circuit had caused her to question every dang little thing. Her confidence shaken, she'd accepted Rodney's invitation to dinner.

While she battled the long, lonely absences of her best friend, she'd let her guard down and spent more time with eager Rodney. He distracted her mind with constant questions of the industry and her work. His promise of sinking in some capital to help her with buying more stock kept her going back for more talks.

He mistook her purely business interest as something far more intimate.

As if! She didn't think of Rodney in that way. Obviously, he did of her.

And that was a huge problem. The minute he had pressed for more—holding her hand, a peck on the cheek—she'd recognized that cow-eyed look.

She took another swig, wetting her parched throat as she watched Cody kicking up his boots, figuring she must have that same look now.

How could this have happened?

They'd been besties since before they could both talk. Their families—friends for ages—set them down in a small, clean corral with fresh hay to play where they shared toys, grew older and bolder, and found ways to escape to wander the McCall ranch.

If Cody didn't think of it first, she did. Off they went, getting into hijinks and trouble. *Still do.*

Back then, it was common knowledge, if someone found one of them, they'd find the other. Even through school, the same occurred.

The feisty music ended and the clapping grew louder. Requests peppered the air as more people sauntered into the bar. At least the night wasn't a total loss.

Hannah watched Cody greet the newcomers, the center where they all gravitated to. It had always been like that. People adored Cody McCall—good-time Cods.

Even through hard times, he'd be the one everyone went to. At fifteen, when his parents died in the cattle stampede, he'd been the hopeful son, where his family and friends turned to and leaned on. His natural ability to brighten up a room got them through the worst of it.

And four years later, Cody had driven over two hundred miles to her college late one night to be the one to tell her that her folks died in a car accident—on their way to secretly getting hitched for the third time. *Two divorces from each other already didn't matter, it seemed.* Cody had gently broken the news, held her while she cried her heart out, helped her pack her things, and then brought her into the McCall fold to plan their funerals and to heal.

Her friend had also been the one to believe in her wild dream of starting her own stock contractor business, even lending her thousands from his own rodeo money to fund it.

"Okay." She blew out a long, slow breath. "It's gratitude. That's all."

The pep talk petered out almost as fast and as soon as she thought it.

Cody drew near. Her pulse kicked up. He crowded in, brushing her leg with his. Tiny thrills scattered along her nerve endings. He grabbed the beer from her hand, tipped it back, and then guzzled the rest down. The long column of his exposed neck fascinated her. Finishing, he smacked his lips and slammed the bottle on the bar behind her.

"Done. Now, it's just you and me, Hannah."

Promises. Promises.

Holding out his hand, he raised an eyebrow. "You game?"

Am I!

She gathered her reserves. Business, making a solid name for herself—and by herself—in the rodeo circuit, remained paramount. Nothing, not even Cody McCall, could shake her from that goal. With her staunch reminder ringing in her mind, Hannah tilted her head back and eyed him. "Me? Ha! I invented the game and won it already, Cods!"

Keep saying it, girl, and maybe you'll start believing it someday.

Chapter Three

CODY SWITCHED OFF the headlights and eased her baby blue, vintage seventies truck to a halt in front of the boarding house. "Hey, Hanns, wake up. We're here."

"I'm not sleeping. Just checking my eyelids." She shoved herself up, hampered by the seat belt he'd secured around her. She let out a burp. The yeasty scent of beer followed.

"Damn, girl, how much did you have to drink, anyway?" She'd tossed back more than he'd counted along with a few extra shots. Strange, she only binge drank when she was worried about something big and scary. Like once or twice in her lifetime before now. For some reason, this time, she hadn't shared with him. Or was it this Rodney fella? No way! She'd never cave in.

If he had the cash he'd loan it to her. *She couldn't be that desperate for funds to agree to Rodney's proposal, could she?*

Flutters of anxiety set flight in his gut. Time away from her cost too much for his liking. Why wasn't she confiding in him now?

Hannah released the buckle and shot a quick peek at the two-story, white clapboard home outlined by the full moon.

A lone night light shone from the first-floor window. "Sneak me in, Cods."

"You live here, don't you?"

"No drinking allowed, remember?" She searched the cab interior and found a half-filled water bottle. Downing the liquid in record time, she tossed the plastic container in the back.

"Come on. They can't be that bad." He ducked his head to eye the darkened top floor. "Miss Peaches and Miss Clementine are snug as a bug in a rug." The Honor sisters owned nearly half the town—even years after their daddy had won it in a poker match, slapped his name on it, and then sold off parcels to fund another gamble—and the only boarding house around.

She chuckled. "They're like hounds, I tell you. Catch me every dang time I come in late."

"Not the curfew still." The older spinster sisters had some strict rules for their boarders. Hannah, gone for weeks at a time on the road, scraped by most days when she was in town.

"You in or what?"

Sighing, he shut down the engine, climbed out of the truck, and then gently shut the door. By the time he made it around the hood, she was face down on the hard ground. "Whoa, girl!"

"Oops!"

Cody rushed to her side, helping her up. She stumbled.

He caught her, dragging her to her wobbly feet.

"Shhh! Don't make any noise." Her loud whisper cut through the night air.

An owl hooted. Crickets chirped. In the distance, he swore he heard a bullfrog croak.

"They'll kick me out for sure if I break another rule. Where else will I go? For a couple hundred a month, this is all I can afford."

"I thought you passed that suspension period."

"For your information, I did, with flying colors. But... I'm on my next one already."

He groaned.

"I know. A grown woman scared to get kicked out of her own rented room. Just a few more months, maybe six or seven, and I can get the ol' Baxter place, house my bulls on my own land, fix the property a bit—"

"That rundown shack?" It would take more than what she had in the bank to remodel the dilapidated house.

"See, I knew you'd understand."

"Not exactly."

"Until then, I need this place So, scoot. Around back. My window's unlocked."

He muttered a curse. How in the world could he get her to go one yard never mind a hundred?

"Don't yell." Cody hauled her over his shoulder.

"Hey!" Her shout pierced the stillness.

"Pipe down." His fierce order was met with a groan.

"My belly hurts."

"Don't puke on me." He hiked her up higher. She barely weighed a hundred pounds soaking wet. "Easy, right?"

Thankfully, she didn't respond to that. He made short work of cutting across the lawn and around the big house. With each step, she made funny noises and began to hiccup. Then she'd giggle. A dog barked, making him jump. Finally, she relaxed, going slack. *Maybe she passed out.* Shrubs cluttered near the base of her window and he wondered how he'd get over them.

Cody jogged the last few feet.

Hannah came to life, thrashing and kicking. "Quit! Stomach. Gonna get sick…" Her left booted foot landed on his upper thigh and too close for comfort.

The sharp pain lanced through him. "Son of a biscuit—" His hold loosened and he dropped her.

Her body hit the solid ground with a dull thud. She moaned. Her hiccups stopped dead in their tracks.

"Hann, I'm sorry. You okay?" He reached for her.

"What are you doing?" She rolled to her knees, scrambling away from him and stumbling to gain her feet and rubbing her stomach.

The barking ripped through the night, on and on like fingers on a chalkboard.

"There's a step stool hiding between the shrub and house. Hurry before they wake up." Her hushed voice rose at the end.

Scowling at her, he gave in and checked. Nothing but branches and dirt greeted him. "It's not there."

Hannah nudged her way through, searching high and low and even raking through the freshly manicured greenery. "What do you mean it's not... Judd must have found it when he cut these. The shed then?"

A light from the third floor came on, spilling from the window.

"No time! Lift me." She bent at the waist.

Before he knew it, he flung off his cowboy hat, ducked, and got behind her. She planted herself on his shoulders. Cody grabbed her thighs and stood. Hannah wrapped her legs behind him and clutched his hair with both her hands.

"Move!" By her tone, she'd grown stone-cold sober. "Cods, it's my last chance. They're going to kick me out. I can't let that happen. Nowhere else..."

"Gotcha." He lurched forward, right into the shrubs. The branches poked and scratched, but he gripped her legs at the same time she squeezed them around his neck. "Damn!"

"Just a little more..." She stretched out, plastering her hands on the window pane. "The hall light just came on. I can see it under the crack in the bottom of the door."

"Shove it open!"

Hannah shifted and Cody staggered. "Almost there." The wood scraping alerted him to the fact she'd gotten it started and pushed it higher. She came off his shoulders, half in the opening. "Cods, grab a handful of my butt and give it all you got. Don't be shy. Just do it!"

Thoughts of "why him" scattered through his mind. He closed his eyes and counted to three. Cody did as she asked, cupping her bottom in his palms. Small, perfectly round... He groaned.

"Now!"

With one last-ditch effort, Cody shoved her up and through the open window.

The crash and her yelps jolted him to plant his hands on the sill and hop up. The sound of his new, blue shirt ripping cut through the silence. His torso cleared the area just as the door banged open and bright light flooded her small, sparsely furnished room.

Hannah gasped.

Cody jerked his head up to find the two sisters—in matching yellow nightgowns and hair in pink rollers—each clutching a shotgun aimed at him. "Miss Peaches. Miss Clementine. Nice evening, isn't it?"

"You git in here," Hannah said between gritted teeth.

"Mr. McCall. What do you have to say for yourself?" Miss Clementine, the older one by two years, didn't drop the barrel.

He hiked himself in the rest of the way, finally placing first one foot and then the other on the wooden floor. The sound of his boots landed with a thud.

Hannah scrambled to her feet, swiping her hands across her jean clad butt.

Glancing at her, he noted her pale face and beautiful brown eyes, round like saucers. Her lips lost all their color, too. A riot of emotions chased over her features, mostly shafts of pain. His heart squeezed tight.

The sisters would certainly toss her out for entertaining a gentlemen under their roof. The breach in their protocol would stain their sterling reputation in town.

Pride and independence served Hannah Prescott since she'd been orphaned as a college student. She'd brushed off help or stood on her own two feet when it came to caring for herself. Heck, he'd had enough of a hard time just getting her to take his investment in her stock years ago.

But right this moment, she needed him more than she ever realized. A wicked idea raced through his mind. It would jolt Gramps out of his doldrums. And he'd save his best friend. He could kill two birds with one stone.

Cody placed an arm around Hannah, tugging her to his side. She fit nicely there, the top of her now wild hairstyle brushing and tickling his jaw. Why hadn't he noticed how perfect they were together before now?

They could benefit from teaming up. He looked at the older ladies, steadfastly aiming at his crotch now. "Miss Peaches. Miss Clementine. My apologizes for announcing myself this way. You'll be pleased as punch to know my intentions are completely honorable."

"What?"

He swore they all spoke at once. Turning to Hannah's

upraised face, his heartbeat stuttered. "Why Hannah here has agreed to be my bride. Isn't that right, sweetheart?"

Leaning in, he stole a kiss. It was supposed to be quick and chaste. However, she bit his bottom lip and jammed her heel down on his foot.

Cody chuckled, pulling her to his chest. He threaded his long fingers through her silky blonde hair and cupped the back of her head. With his lips brushing hers, he murmured, "Why, yes indeed. The future Mrs. McCall is one heck of a spitfire. I wouldn't want it any other way."

Chapter Four

HANNAH'S MIND REELED with the implications. *Say it ain't so!*

"This can't be happening." She shot Miss Peaches and Miss Clementine a weak smile as they threw question after question at her in their prim and proper formal living room. The red Victorian couch and stiff back chairs were comfy compared to their intense interrogation.

It was rather ridiculous to see the sisters in their granny gowns, thick slipper socks in neon orange planted on their expensive antique oriental rug of reds and creams. That was not forgetting the rollers in their hair and rifles laying across their laps as they fondly stroked the metal barrels like a pampered kitty cat. Somehow, Hannah never imagined she'd see them in anything shy of their Sunday best while entertaining in their pristine parlor.

They were, to say the least, the most eccentric landlords—a foot each in a different century—this town had ever had the grace to witness. Their wealthy daddy had left the sisters an oil well or a half dozen and most of the town, so they'd never worked a day in their lives. However, they certainly took great pleasure in influencing the townspeople with their generous offerings whenever they could.

Who could say no to them? Who had ever said no to the dynamic sisters?

Hannah groaned inwardly. One bad word from either one and she'd never find a decent place to bunk down. Where would she live? She didn't have the money to buy anything just yet, not for months to come. *For her or for her stock.* The Barclays were rather fond of the sisters. And would her lease for the land and pens for her bulls with the Barclays disappear, too?

Moving, finding a new home, and the huge task of resettling dropped on her shoulders like a mad, two-ton bull.

An image of her money being sucked out an open window flashed through her mind.

"It's been a rumor for years, my dear. You and Cody just had to grow up a bit." Miss Peaches' brows drew down hard and quick. "Although, it didn't appear you have grown up at all from tonight's shenanigans."

"Sneaking in your bedroom window at three in the morning? Really?" Miss Clementine scowled. "Why, it's a wonder you didn't wake the entire town. Thank goodness, we don't have all our rooms full and our dear cousin, Mr. Samuels, is away on business and didn't have to witness this…this catastrophe."

Her head pounded. Mixing beer and whiskey together did not sit well. The aftereffects sat hard and heavy in her belly like a sharp-sided rock. Or was that what shock felt like?

They'd kicked Cody out over an hour ago, so she sat facing them on her own. Her palms grew damp and she swiped them along her jeans. She gulped hard at the reminder that Cody's warm, wide hands had gripped her in that very spot, his fingertips imprinted there, too, and in more intimate places she begged him to touch.

"Aren't you two tired?" Hannah yawned, trying to get them to back down. Maybe if they slept it off, they'd be persuaded to dismiss her giant blunder. "We can take this up in the morning. Or Sunday, before church. Forgiveness and all. And dear Mr. Samuels can come back to his room with peace and quiet in the house." *And because I have to go over how it went from bad to worse. Then figure out a way to fix it.*

Cody McCall had done the unthinkable. Not only had he thrown fuel on the fire with her strict, uptight landlords, but he'd up and kissed her. Like a real, live, hot kiss!

Her lips still tingled. The only satisfaction she gained from the entire experience was that she'd let him know in no uncertain terms, she did not like to be manhandled or manipulated.

She seemed to mock herself at that little, white lie. Cody McCall lived up to everything she'd ever heard regarding his much-talked about incredible abilities to make women swoon. Pleasure prickled over her skin and slid down her spine. She suppressed the shiver.

"What are we to do?" Miss Clementine, older and more prim, directed the question at Hannah and not Miss Peaches.

"We? Do?" Hannah jerked her head from one sister to the other. Stony silence met her desperate inquiry. "Oh, as in *me* do it." This changed things.

The scenario went something like, the one in the hot seat would come up with a few suggestions, each met with a blank stare. If one spotted a raised eyebrow by both sisters at the same time, why, that was what they would ultimately do to take their penitence and be done with it. Somehow, they'd always cornered her into doing more time and hardship than she'd figured.

"I'm sorry? Go back to the way things were?" They seemed to stare harder. *Nope, not that one.* "Ahh…try not to do it again? Never, ever let Cody back in the house?" *Crickets.* "No engagement?" The air throbbed. "Marry him?" She blurted out the most difficult choice, yet the one most accepted.

The sisters' eyebrows shot up as if four gray caterpillars came to life. Miss Clementine's sigh, hot and heavy, sailed through the air.

"No!"

"It's the only way, dear." Miss Peaches, the softer, kinder sister, gave her a little shrug and pasted on a smile.

What had she done to deserve this wicked punishment?

CODY EASED HANNAH'S borrowed truck to a halt in front of the long, low ranch house snuggled in behind the wraparound porch and shut the engine down.

Gray dawn streaked the sky above and beyond. He figured he could sneak into his room upstairs and clean up before anyone, especially Gramps, realized he'd been gone all night.

Maybe he'd saddle up his horse, Ginger, and ride fast and hard to catch the sunrise. He needed open space to process what he'd gone and done. If it weren't about her, he'd have sought out his best friend Hannah for her advice.

By noon the news would be all over town.

Something in his gut clutched, hard and quick. He sucked in a breath and then another one. Hannah? He'd kissed *his* Hannah.

And it felt damn good, too.

Darts of desire plucked at his nerve endings. His lips were imprinted with the feel of her soft, lush ones. She tasted like whiskey and beer and cotton candy, a very heady combination in his book. Stunned wonder rippled through him at the sudden realization.

Cody McCall wanted more from Hannah Prescott.

He gulped. His hands shook.

Getting out of the truck, he gently closed the door, hearing the soft click. He dragged his booted feet across the dusty driveway and up the walkway. With his head down, he climbed the steps to the porch.

"Mighty late, aren't you?" The familiar, deep voice sliced through the gray shadows. He nudged his foot, setting the wooden rocker in motion as he sat deep in his favorite spot.

Cody stilled in his tracks. "Gramps." It came out part sigh and part shock. *Caught. Again.* But this time there'd be hell to pay. Staring harder, he made out the outline of his grandfather, fully dressed and with his worn Stetson pushed back on his head. His constant companion these days sat at his feet. The white miniature horse lifted his head. "Must not have won if you're still up."

"Don't sleep much anymore, son." The rest of his unfinished explanation hung thick and heavy between them. Not since his beloved wife had died.

There were more words to come. Cody waited. He tugged off his cowboy hat and then set it on the nearby rail. With unsteady fingers, he brushed his wayward hair off his forehead.

"Miss Peaches called."

"Ah, hell!" The weight of it pressed on his shoulders.

"So, it's true."

"What part are we talking about?" *Could he buy some time?* He leaned against the porch post, arms crossed over his chest, and one booted foot over the other.

"Drunk?"

"Yep."

"Crawling through the bedroom window?"

"Well, if you put it like that, yes, sir." *How could he deny it?* "Sounds worse than it seemed."

"Kissing little Hannah?"

"She's a grown woman." His throat closed up. *And what a woman! Feisty spitfire!* An ache shot through him. He grit his teeth.

How could he have feelings for her after all this time? He swore he'd keep his heart intact and out of harm's way after his misguided mess with Tabitha last year. Cody couldn't figure out women and didn't have any inclinations to do so either.

"You gonna finish it or me?" Gramps slow drawl held a hint of a smile in it.

Cody perked up at the first sign of life in his grandfather in ages. "You can do the honors."

"Seems to me like we've got a wedding to plan, son. Is that about right?"

"Could be." An image of digging himself deeper in a six-foot ditch flashed through his mind. Hannah would most likely oversee his demise to finish him off, too.

"Hot dang! Your Grams is dancing a jig right about now!" Gramps sniffed.

Cody's throat closed up.

"That's all we ever wanted for you boys. Nothing sweeter than seeing your grandsons find true love and settle down to start a family. We dreamed about you and your brothers finding what we had. Yes, sirree!" He shoved himself out of the chair and practically did a two-step all the way to the front door. The horse followed his master, clip-clopping over the wooden planks.

Straightening away from the post, Cody's mouth gaped open. "Gramps?" *Was his grandfather back? Is that what it took? A grandson's wedding?*

"Now I got something to fight for. I'll be damned if that bank steals our ranch out from under us!" He stuck a thumb to his chest. "They've never been up against a McCall before. Just watch me!"

With more gusto than Cody had seen in over a year—since his grandmother's diagnosis—he watched Gramps storm into the house.

A shot of adrenaline rushed through Cody's blood. He whistled low. *Hannah, honey, I hope you're up for this ride we're about to take. Nothing's gonna stop me from making Gramps the happiest man in the county.*

Life as he knew it would never be the same.

Chapter Five

FORTY MINUTES LATER, freshly showered, wearing clean clothes, and with wet hair, Cody entered the long, cozy, country blue kitchen. Gramps stood at the counter with a mixing bowl, a flat of eggs, and a loaf of bread in front of him.

His pet horse reclined on his handmade quilt bed in the corner. With his food untouched in special pristine-white, ceramic bowls with his name carefully painted on them, Gramps shook his head. "Go on and eat up now, Sweet Potato."

"Where's Caleb and Conner?" His brothers were early risers and came for breakfast nearly every day.

"Our sheriff took an extra shift today." He waved a large, wooden spoon to a spot beyond the big window, revealing the yellow and orange sun over the horizon. "And Connor's filling in for Juan, feeding the horses."

"Ah, his name is *Johnny*." He chuckled. *How many times could he correct him before he got it straight?*

"I like Juan better."

"He and Rose should be back tomorrow, right?" The

sweet, quiet middle-aged couple had taken care of them for the last few years. Their devotion to Grams during her illness and all the McCalls then and since would never be forgotten.

"Rosa."

"Gramps, it's *Rose*." He shook his head at his grandfather's set ways.

"She's Rosa to me."

"Suit yourself." He eyed the big stove. An empty cast iron pan on top with the flame burning under it to warm it sat there. "Your turn or mine?"

"Whattya have, son?"

"French toast?" His hopes grew at the prospect of having one of his favorites and not eating his own lame attempts at cooking.

"Eggs, it is."

He groaned inwardly. "Second choice, I guess. Fried."

"Scrambled." Gramps cracked several eggs, one right after the other, and plopped them in the big, blue ceramic bowl. He whisked them, the spoon clattering against the side of the bowl.

"Whatever you say."

"You got that, son." He smiled.

"Grams was right, you like doing things your way."

"Always have. Always will."

Pulling out a chair at the long, scarred oak table, Cody sank down in the tall, ladder back seat. The large kitchen and dining room, once filled with boisterous comings and goings, echoed with ghosts of the past. He longed to hear his Grams giving his Gramps a lecture on his cooking techniques as she washed dirty dishes in the big farm sink.

Even so, the normalcy of the morning routine seemed at complete odds with the life changing events of last night.

He wondered how Hannah was doing. The sisters surely had cornered her and grilled her before Miss Peaches called Gramps in the early morning hours.

After this, he'd go to her. *What would he say?* His heartbeat stuttered. What would facing her again be like? How could he have reunited with her as best friends Friday night and a short time later left her as something more?

That more part, yeah, that's going to be a sticking point with her.

The sizzle of the liquid hitting the hot pan brought Cody back to the moment. He watched as Gramps stirred, keeping up with the fast-cooking eggs.

Within minutes, he plated part of the finished meal, grabbed a couple of slices of toast, and then set it down in front of Cody.

A fusion of surprise lanced through him as his grandfather reached for a small plate and heaped a mound of scrambled eggs on it and settled in opposite Cody. "You joining me?" *He's eating?*

"Nothing like a wedding to look forward to." After splashing on a wide arch of pepper, he hunkered down and ate.

A stab of guilt poked at Cody. "I have to discuss the details with…Hannah." Her name stuck in the back of his throat. Everything had changed.

What was she feeling?

Skittish at anything romantic, Hannah had made her ideas known over the years. She was not the marrying kind. Nope, she didn't want to end up pining for someone who didn't pine right back for her.

"Miss Peaches and Miss Clementine should be along with her any minute now."

Cody shoved back, planting his palms on the edge of the table. "Whoa! Can't do it. The ranch. I have chores to do." He jerked his gaze to the back door and then to the window over the sink. "Lots of them. All day."

"Simmer down. Conner's filling in, I told you."

"He knows? Caleb?" Cody's belly clenched.

Sheriff Caleb McCall could detect the slightest hesitation when he interrogated someone, especially with him when he'd been up to no good growing up. Things were getting more complicated.

"Not exactly." He sipped his steaming mug of black coffee. "Good stuff." Gramps smacked his lips. He waved a hand back and forth between them. "Alone time. I guess they figured we could catch up."

Like a clock ticking away in his ear, Cody felt the pressure to confess. "Gramps, there's something you should know—"

A loud knock sounded on the front door. Another one followed.

"That's them." Gramps jumped to his feet and swaggered down the hallway. Sweet Potato bolted up and sauntered after his master.

Cody rushed to keep up. "Wait! I'll get it." Maybe he could head them off, delay the outcome, before he could convince Hannah to go along.

Surprisingly, Gramps moved faster than usual and yanked open the door. "Hello, ladies!"

"Yoo-hoo!" Miss Peaches burst over the threshold, followed by her sister, who dragged a mutinous Hannah by the arm.

"My, aren't you the prettiest things in your matching, bright green dresses! And look at my future granddaughter, Hannah." He gave her a swift, crushing hug.

"Gramps." She plastered on a grim smile before shooting Cody with a fierce glare. "Why if it isn't the traitor himself!"

She narrowed her stare, pinning him with those gorgeous brown eyes. Steaming mad would be too mild a word to describe her.

Oh, hell!

HANNAH RODE AHEAD on the gray mare. The stray heads of cattle and longhorns mooed and scattered. The galloping thunder of the strong horse beneath her and the wind blasting her face and through her hair swept away the cobwebs from her mind.

Her troubling thoughts slipped away.

This, the land, the earth centered her. The majestic animal carrying her brought home the gratitude of all things beautiful on the McCall ranch.

It was here on this lush green grass she'd learned how to crawl, walk, run over the hills, and ride as her parents worked with the McCalls breeding a new type of cow—sturdier and stronger—to survive the rugged winters and drought-ridden, scorching hot summers. Hand in hand, the friends toiled away at their dreams.

Her father had come and gone from the rodeo circuit to pitch in, even after the first divorce, which led to the second marriage, and so on. *Hot and cold.*

And in a flash, all was lost when Cody's parents died that day...

He'd seen it all unfold.

She swallowed hard at the gripping wave of pain. *For him. For all of them.* Hannah eased back on the reins, directing the horse to a slow trot. In the distance, she heard Cody's horse's pounding hooves following her.

A smile tugged up the corner of her mouth. He didn't need a GPS to know she'd come to her favorite strand of trees.

"Easy, girl." Her whispered words and gentle tug on the

reins directed the mare to a halt. Hannah swung off and dropped to the hard ground, nudging the horse to nibble on the blades of new grass nearby.

Under the huge oak tree now, Hannah sank to the ground, propping herself against the thick trunk and hugging her knees to her chest. She watched as Cody and his horse flew like the wind over the land and toward her. She would know that man anywhere.

Her heart skipped a beat and then another. *How could this happen to her of all people?*

Hannah didn't want to feel anything ever again; it hurt too damn much to love people. They'd let her down.

Bulls, raising them and training there, were her life. As unpredictable as they were, they were far more stable than Cody McCall ever would be.

His wild streak sparked a kinship with her. Carefree and kicking up fun served them well all this time. *Why change that now?*

"Yeah, heart, tell me that?" Her muttered words died in her mouth when he halted a few feet away and jumped down from his horse.

Cody swatted the horse's rump. "Go on now. Rest up." He turned to her, his endearing features expressionless. But his eyes, green and burning bright, slammed into her. "You ever think we'd be plunked down in the middle of crazy? You and me?" He turned his head away, searching the ridge. He pointed. "Just yesterday I was there riding home. All I wanted was a cold beer and to kick up my boots to a few lively tunes at The Giddy Up."

"And look what you got." She finished it for him. They'd done that for ages, too. "How do we turn this wreck around, Cods?" *How do I stop my heart from aching for you? Or is it just that my body is craving you?*

He sauntered over and plopped himself down. His arm brushed hers.

She sucked in a sharp, painful breath at the zap of barely contained lightning. *No, stop that!*

Cody stilled.

Hannah clamped her eyes shut for a second. *He felt it, too!*

Gingerly, he shifted until he rested his arm on one raised knee. He plucked up a blade of grass and chewed on it.

He held out his hands as if cupping something. "You got a nice butt."

Of all the things he could have said, he'd gone and said that. Hannah smacked his forearm and chuckled. Cody joined in until they were both laughing out loud. The tension between them siphoned out in a whoosh.

"That's my girl. That's my Hannah." What should have come out as lighthearted came out on a wistful note.

She sobered quickly. "Yours ain't bad, either." Hannah's face grew warm. "You know, when you're dancing I sorta noticed."

"Good to know there's that." He gulped loud enough for

her to hear. "Gramps…he's happy." He waved his thumb toward her and then to himself. "About us."

"That so." She pressed her forehead against her upraised knees. "God, Cods. I never thought…not us. Do we have to do this? I mean, go through with it?"

"What? You mean pretend?" His voice seemed hopeful.

Hannah jerked her head up and twisted to look directly at him. His eyebrows lifted and his green eyes held doubt and a ray of hope. Reaching over, she plucked the blade of grass from between his slack lips and tossed it away. If only she could kiss him again. This time she'd take what she wanted.

"They're planning our wedding—just shy of a shotgun one. How are we going to pull this off, Hann?"

She loved when he looked at her that way—as if she were his world. *Wow, did I just think that?* She loved when he called her his Hannah or Hann. Something hard and sharp tugged behind her ribs. "Fake engagement?" Her breath hitched.

"We can drag it out, right? A long, long time. The newness will wear off. In the meantime, it will stop Rodney in his tracks, you get to stay at Miss Peaches and Miss Clementine's boarding house, it gives Gramps something to look forward to until he's back on his feet, and we'll always be best friends no matter what. Perfect."

Nodding as he spoke, she followed the movement of his lips. He'd tasted so good right before she reacted with that little nibble.

"Practice." As his brows came down, she rushed to explain. "You want this to look natural to everyone. Like we're a real couple. All the stages, from bestowed to irritated and everything in between. We have to fool them."

A streak of concern chased across his eyes. "You mean lie, don't you?" Cody blew out a warm breath. "I can't do that to Gramps."

Would it be lying on her part? "No, of course not." She swallowed past the lump in her parched throat. "It helps we like each other. People already think there's something going on." Hannah shrugged. "We play that up. It means spending more time together. And, uh, maybe, a kiss or two." *I just need to get this and us out of my system, that's all. Once that's done, we can go back to the way things were. Yeah, right!*

A fresh blast of warmth flooded her cheeks. She dropped her stare to his lips again. Hannah licked hers.

"Can we do that, Cods?" She gazed up at him, capturing his glance. Heat flashed in his green eyes, spending sparks galloping in her veins.

He leaned forward, inch by agonizingly slow inch. Cody halted a hairsbreadth away. "Hannah Prescott, will you be my pretend bride-to-be?"

"Yeah, Cods. I'm yours." And she meant it more than he would ever know.

At last, he brushed his firm lips against hers.

The touch, light and tender, melted her.

Cody threaded his fingers through her hair, cupping the back of her head in his hand. He tilted up her chin and deepened the slow, seductive kiss.

He tasted sweet and sinful at the same time. Her head spun. Her toes tingled. And Hannah's resistance—if there were any left to speak of—plunged over a dizzying cliff.

She increased the pressure, aching with the need flooding her body.

Yep, she liked it. Way too much! Now, how in tarnation was she ever going to walk about from this heady rush…

Chapter Six

CODY COULD BARELY think at the riotous feelings still rushing through his body from Hannah's mind-boggling kiss yesterday. He'd done everything in his power to erase the thrilling, yet disturbing, sensations by hauling bales of hay to brushing down the horses to carrying buckets of feed. Nothing worked. *Not. A. Damn. Thing.*

Standing in the middle of the impromptu barbecue slash engagement party at the McCall ranch after church on Sunday, he barely recognized his lively grandfather. He barked out orders to Caleb manning the six-foot-long smoker and joked with family and friends, making sure they had enough grub to eat and beer to drink from the nearby kegs. The hint of smoke clung to the air from the slabs of brisket and racks of ribs cooking.

Rose and Johnny, having returned from their little geta-way to San Antonio, lent a hand, serving the swelling crowd of at least sixty. More were streaming in to the huge back-yard, carrying their specialty covered dishes. Word traveled fast, especially when Gramps stood up in church and made the announcement hours ago.

Cody still cringed at the gasps and standing ovation Hannah and he had received from the good people of their hometown. She'd ducked her head and clutched his hand as they both winced. Lying didn't sit well and if felt much, much worse in the house of worship. Being stared at intently by the pastor didn't help matters any, either.

"Yo, brother." Connor—younger and leaner—came up beside Cody and slapped a hand on his shoulder. "Congrats! I knew there was something between you and Hannah. Can't hide love, can you?"

"Guess not." Maybe he and Hannah could practice some pat answers to feed people later. *Prefer practicing kisses more, though.* Shock lanced through his mind. *Why now? Why ever?* The one thing he didn't want to lose in his life besides his grandfather and brothers was his best friend Hannah. *No!* But the swift ache at that scary thought rushed to his chest.

He found her squarely planted among his grandmother's various flower gardens—tended to now by Rose and his aunt—with the church ladies and Miss Peaches on one side and Miss Clementine on the other. From here, he could only imagine Hannah rolling her eyes in disgust. His grin came easy.

"Who would have thought you'd be the first McCall brother to tie the knot? My bet was on Caleb all along." Conner nodded to their oldest brother. "Thought the sheriff would sign up someone to fulfill that post."

They chuckled. Their brother, always the leader, returned from the military four years ago more determined than ever to serve his community. He'd won the election hands down and continued to keep all of them in order.

"Got a date in mind yet?" Conner sipped his beer. "Gramps can't stop smiling. Good job on that." Relief washed over his features, smoothing out the worry lines there.

That's what they all wanted, wasn't it? To make Gramps happy. "Look, Aunt Sissy, Uncle Jeb, and the cousins just arrived." He smiled at his tiny aunt—decked out in her fancy yellow cowgirl hat, matching shirt and boots, and wearing jeans—as she greeted her big brother. Left McCall, tall and barrel-chested, towered over his little sister. Twenty years and over a foot difference in height didn't matter much to the adopted siblings. He gave her a bear hug before greeting his tall, slim brother-in-law and three rowdy nephews.

"Fried chicken?" Connor eyed the platters their Laramie cousins carried. "Let's see, Jacob must have that one. Jackson, hmmm?"

"That green bean casserole, I hope." Cody's stomach growled. He hadn't eaten a dang thing since Gramps' scrambled eggs yesterday morning. If anything could get him hungry again, it would be Aunt Sissy's cooking.

"Surely, she made her pecan pie? Jordan? Uncle Jeb?" He shut one eye and zeroed in on them. "Definitely, Uncle." He pointed to their grandfather now ruffling Dwight Marsh's little boy's dark hair. "The sooner the better for you to tie the knot and pop out great grands for him."

All of them had been worried. Grams' passing had left a huge hole in the family and nearly crippled their Gramps. They'd done almost anything and everything to bring him back from the depths of his overwhelming grief.

But kids? Don't push it! Beads of sweat rolled down his temple. He swiped them away. "What about you, little bro?" He diverted the attention away from himself.

"Me? No way. I'm going to get some fried chicken and stop this line of questioning." He smacked Cody on his chest and walked away, backward. "Don't even breathe a word of that pile of crap around me!" Conner turned and ran smack into Julie Garcia. He jerked back, lifting his hands and his bottle high. "Sorry."

"Save me a dance, Connor!" She planted her hands on her hips as he rushed away.

Before she turned back, Cody went around the table with the mountain of desserts piled on it and headed to his pretend bride.

The buzz was back—women jabber jawing about flowers—perhaps even from Grams' own gardens—showers, and wedding gowns. His Hannah, pale and shaking, stood in the center, nodding numbly at the suggestions. *Skittish? More like she's going to bolt any minute now!*

"Ladies, ladies, please give her some air." Cody shouldered his way through.

He found her looking all sweet and sexy in her little red

sundress and matching cowgirl boots. Something tugged, low and deep. He shook his head, wondering when that had started. *This was Hannah, for crying out loud!*

But his body didn't listen. It hummed. Cody pressed forward, halting by her side. He tucked a sweep of her hair behind her ear. Her frown vanished. In its place, she shot him a grateful smile. She lost that scared look and he thought his knees would buckle at the way she stared up at him with those soulful brown eyes of hers.

Cody wrapped an arm around her and tugged her close, dropping a gentle kiss on her forehead.

Several gasps floated to him and a few ahhs. His gesture surprised them as much as it did him.

What's happening to you, McCall?

"Thanks, Cods." Her whispered words pushed away his lingering doubts. He'd eased her anxiety. It was the least he could do for her.

"I'm stealing my girl, ladies. Any complaints take them up with the sheriff over there."

Hannah giggled.

His insides jumped and then stuttered. "Girl, I wouldn't do that if I were you."

"What's that?" She clasped his hand, yanking him away from the middle of the highly excitable, chattering women, around the gardens, and to the lively, growing bunch waiting on them.

"Forget it." He didn't want to explain the strange reactions he was having to his best friend. "Beer?"

"Dance with me first, cowboy." She yanked his hat off his head and reached up with her other hand, mussing up his hair.

This time he laughed. She was the only one he'd ever let do that to him.

She plunked down his hat on her head, shifting it toward the back and grinned up at him, slow and sexy.

An image of her in nothing but his cowboy hat and her red cowgirl boots slammed into him. Cody shivered and then blew out a hot breath. "That's a mighty fine invitation." His voice dropped to a husky note.

This time she gasped, biting her lip.

Gunther strummed his guitar, the first notes met by a loud cheer. The makeshift dance floor began to fill up.

Cody ignored the snappy tune and leaned toward Hannah. This wasn't playacting; he felt and saw her quiver just before he claimed her soft, sweet lips. She sighed. He moaned.

A brief thought flashed across his mind. *God, this is going to be hell extracting us out of this mess in the end...*

DIZZY, HANNAH'S HEAD swam—not with anything she'd drank, because she hadn't had anything stronger than a cola all night—but with Cody McCall. She leaned her head on his shoulder as they swayed to the touching ballad.

Night had fallen. The string of white lights surrounding Grams' garden twinkled. She'd danced with nearly everyone there at least once, one by one or in groups like with her girlfriends. Always, she'd returned to an eager Cody.

Dang, but he could dance, sweeping her off her feet or swinging her around or just holding her close like this.

She pressed a hand to his chest, feeling the heavy thump of his heartbeat against her palm. Awe rushed through her. *She'd done that to him.*

His scent, clean and all male, filled her senses.

Hannah sighed. A shudder went through him. An answering quiver tickled her spine.

This was so wrong, but oh, so right.

For all these years, for all the speculation they drew when they danced, finally she could slip into his arms and relax into his strength, his protection. *Safe. Home.*

In this moment, he was hers and she was his.

That was heady and thrilling and scary all at the same time.

Like a drug, she wanted more.

If only…

"RESTRICTION?" HANNAH EYED Miss Peaches and Miss Clementine as they directed her to their old jalopy. The burgundy color shone in the flood light from the McCall's front porch. The dang thing took up nearly half a block in town.

"Yes, dear. Until the wedding." Miss Clementine lifted her chin a notch higher. "Isn't that right, Mr. McCall?"

Gramps swept off his cowboy hat and scratched his head. "Now, Missy, don't you think you've known me long enough to call me Left?"

"Hmph! Why your adopted parents couldn't think of a better name for you then Left is beyond me. Just because you were left on their doorstep when you were a little baby isn't a good enough reason to me."

"Yep, that was Mama and Papa for you. Hearts of gold, mind you. But bad with names. Couldn't think of a better one for their baby girl than name her Sissy. Darnedest thing, isn't it? But they were good to me and I'll always be grateful to them for taking me in. Now, about Hannah and my boy..."

"Am I in trouble again?" Hannah gazed at Cody, shrugging. *What did I do to deserve this?*

"It's proper. He can court you just like any other gentleman does a lady." Miss Peaches leaned forward. "In our presence, of course. After all, we are like your aunties."

"That I pay for room and board." Her voice rose.

"Easy, Hann." Cody slipped an arm around her shoulder. "Excuse us." He tugged her away and on to the porch.

She sank down on the rail. "It was easier when we were

just friends. I could come and go as I pleased, well, within reason. And I could meet up with you anywhere, anytime. One little change and this! It's like living in the dark ages, Cods."

"Maybe it's for the best." He held up his hand when she went to speak. "Just for now. We do as they say, let them breathe easy, and then we nudge back that curfew time of yours." He shook his head in wonder.

Hannah crossed her arms over her chest, hugging herself. "I've got a few more days of this, then I can escape Thursday. I'm going to Flat Rock. Doug Eastman and his men want to see Macho in action. Test him out for a bigger tour. If I can just get him to the big show... Come with me." An ache swirled, low and deep.

His smile lingered and grew. "Very naughty. I like it, though. I'll sneak out and leave Gramps a note. Swing by at dawn to pick me up. He'll keep it hush-hush. You know, that true love stuff he likes to talk about."

She gulped hard. "I'm spending the night. One room or two?" Hannah held her breath for his answer.

Chapter Seven

BEING TIED DOWN to Miss Peaches and Miss Clementine's rules put a crimp in Cody's style. The more they kept him away from Hannah, the more ways they thought of seeing each other.

Like Monday, inviting him to a fancy pot roast dinner, only to have him watch Mr. Samuels—white mustached and bearded gentlemen in a three-piece suit—and the sisters play a mean round of charades. *Thankfully, it wasn't scrabble!*

Hannah saved them both by pleading a toothache and practically shoved him out the door by eight. Strange how he backtracked around the house and wanted to talk to her some more. She'd reluctantly shooed him away for fear of being caught, half hanging out her window with promises of a so-called date.

Too bad the meddling sisters had caught them trying to go to the movies alone tonight. He was a grown man, escorting his intended, along with her chaperones, to see the latest action adventure flick at the lone movie theater in town. It was not his idea of a fun night.

For a Tuesday, there were more of his friends waiting to

get in then he thought possible. He grimaced at the attention Hannah and he were getting and the snickers.

Hannah elbowed him. "Got anything? Anything at all?"

She looked cute making that funny face and rolling her eyes. And she looked even cuter with that new, short teal dress she had on. It was more like an oversized shirt with the turquoise and silver belt riding low on her small hips. A tiny clutch in his belly warned him not to go there.

He tried to look away. His glance skimmed her from head to toe. *Wrong move.* Cody's heartbeat picked up speed. Hannah might deny it, but she had legs that put other girls to shame. He should know; he'd felt them around him.

Sucking in a sharp breath, he caught a whiff of her perfume—heady and sexy—just like her. *Whoa, McCall! Easy does it here!*

"Cods, do something." She smiled through gritted teeth.

"Are you sure about this, ma'am? Your weak tummy and all." He nodded to Miss Peaches, the more reasonable sister.

"Oh, my!" She touched her cheek with one of her white-gloved hands. With yellow flowers sprouting out of her straw bonnet, she could have arrived from a different century. "Will it be that bad, dear?'

"Could be."

"Clementine, I'm not sure about this…"

"We're going." Her sister's staunch reply halted any more objections. In a matching outfit, shades of the same lavender, Miss Clementine hiked up her straw purse on her arm and glared at Cody.

He groaned inwardly. She knew what he'd tried to do. *Mutiny!*

New arrivals rushed to catch up with the moviegoers, now heading for the just opened door of the cinema. Boots scuffed the sidewalk and excited murmurs rose in anticipation. The mouth-watering scent of freshly popped popcorn drifted to him.

His cousin Jacob spotted him in line. "Yo, Cody! Seriously? Hot dates?" He grinned impishly as he ribbed him.

"Payback, cuz, payback." He shot him a narrowed-eyed gaze. An idea began to form. He'd gotten Jacob out of more than one hot spot previously, especially with Uncle Jeb and Aunt Sissy. *Would his cousin go along? And could Cody pull it off?*

"HUNKER DOWN. LOWER." He slid down in his seat and instructed Hannah to do the same.

Leaning close and pressing into his forearm, she whispered, "What for?" She glimpsed over his shoulder. "Nice seats, Miss Clementine, Miss Peaches. Smack dab in the middle. Are you sure you want to sit behind us? Cody's tall. You might not be able to see."

"We're fine, dear." Miss Peaches went back to gingerly removing her gloves, tugging each finger in precise increments.

Cody gulped. Hannah's sweet breath tickled his cheek and with her upper body draped over his arm, he could barely think. "Follow my lead." His low voice shook.

"When? Now?"

"Give it ten minutes in and—" He jerked his head to make certain Miss Clementine stayed engaged with her sister, bickering over the big tub of popcorn. "Jacob agreed. Switch." *That and fifty bucks coerced his cousin to riding this through.*

Somehow, she got the gist. "Ohhhh!" Her beautiful brown eyes grew big and her mouth dropped open a tad.

A low curl of heat tugged inside him.

The lights dimmed. The chatter slammed to a halt. The music grew louder and the screen flashed with the trailer for another movie.

Cody slunk down in the seat even more. His heart thumped louder and louder as the time drew near. The larger-than-life images on the screen held most everyone's rapt attention.

If he weren't so hyped up on escaping his guards, he'd have loved to watch this one.

Swallowing hard, he squeezed Hannah's hand. He eased down and out of the seat. Her fingers snagged the back of his jean belt loop as he led the way. Squatting like a dang duck, he waddled down the row, murmuring his apologizes for both of them. When he got to the last two seats, he tagged his cousin's leg, who in turn tapped Sandy's—his date for the night.

"Got ya."

Jacob's hushed voice sent a flicker of panic through Cody. He prayed the sisters hadn't heard the accompanying shushes from several people around them.

As if in sync, Cody and Hannah slid pass his cousin and his date. They barely got by before Jacob directed Sandy to go first and the duo squatted down until they slipped into Cody and Hannah's seats, hunching down low.

A beat or a half dozen fired in his head before he realized the sisters didn't have a clue.

In the darkened aisle, Cody stayed low, with Hannah behind him as they turned the corner of the wall and tiptoed the rest of the way to the door. He inched it open, the light spilling and leaving an arch.

Hannah scooted through and he scraped by, easing the door closed behind him.

"Phew! We did it!" She hugged him, pressing fully into him.

If anything, the pounding in his chest hammered faster and louder. "We're not in the clear yet." He reached for her hand, palms touching and linking fingers. *Hers were so small and delicate in his.* He gulped hard. "Jacob let me borrow his truck."

"Where we going?" She tugged him toward the exit, ready to bolt.

"You hungry? I'm starving. I skipped Caleb and Gramps' chicken fried steak dinner to get to town on time."

They burst through the glass doors at the same time, drawing in big lungful's of fresh air.

Hannah turned to him and chuckled. "We're free! Pizza, burgers, fries?"

"The Grub Hub it is then." He smiled at the delight written all over her face.

"Cods, I gotta hand it to you. You are a genius." She looked up and down the parked vehicles lining the street. "Which way?"

"Over a block, he said." Cody jerked his head to behind him and they hustled off in that direction.

"His new truck? Sandy says it's got a lot of horse power—get up and go in seconds."

"From his rodeo winnings. Pretty awesome, if you ask me." There was a hint of envy in his gut. If Cody hadn't dropped out last year when Grams had gotten sick, he'd have led in the bareback bronc riding points.

"You did the right thing, Cods." She must have sensed his thoughts. "You can't put dollar signs on the time you got to spend with Grams and your family."

When they reached the shiny blue, four-door truck, she halted at the passenger door. Looking up at him with those big, brown eyes—soft and tender—his heart melted. "Hann…"

"I think you were her favorite. At least that's how I saw

it." She blinked. "Come on, let's shake a leg here. I've got a hole in my stomach that needs filling."

Her sudden light mood didn't fool him. She'd gotten all teary on him.

Cody McCall did not do emotional. He stayed far, far away from the mushy, sharing stuff women liked. He'd rather face a hissing, ten-foot rattlesnake than discuss his feelings.

Hannah knew that. She'd abided by that ninety-nine percent of the time. Heck, she practically invented it herself, choosing to tough it through. At least, most of the time. That one percent included the harsh, gripping reality of first losing his parents and then hers.

A lump formed in his throat.

He assisted her in the high truck since the dress she wore didn't quite cover everything when she hitched up her booted foot on the running board. The material fell away and he got more than a glimpse of those lean thighs of hers again.

Beads of sweat gathered under his collar. His hands, on her waist, dipped to her hips as she shifted higher. A jolt of longing swept through Cody.

She stilled for a brief moment, jerking her gaze over her shoulder to catch and hold his stare. "Did you just...? I mean, like feel something, too?"

"Couldn't be, right?" He shrugged it off.

"'Course not." She made a sound in the back of her

throat.

When she finally got in all the way and he shut the door, Cody rounded the hood of the truck, his hands shaking.

What's happened to us?

Chapter Eight

H ANNAH SETTLED IN the long, high-backed wooden booth in the charming stone building. On the walls hung ancient farm tools and relics and black and white photos of cowboys on the range—several were of the McCalls rounding up cattle and one was of her straddling her first pony when she was just a little girl with her parents on either side of her in happier times. It made her feel closer to them here somehow.

Cody slid in opposite her.

"You sure sitting in front of the big window is the best thing to do?" With the low-hanging, overhead light they were open and exposed to anyone outside.

"Bird's eye view." He leaned forward and crooked his head to gaze down the lane and around the corner to the theater. "Well, if you just bend and twist a tad."

His voice held a smile and it made her breathe easier. They were back on solid footing again. *What was going on with them? If felt like she'd caught some kind of bug or something. Hot. Cold. Jittery. Heavy breathing.*

"Usual?" He glanced at the menu before checking with

her.

His green eyes meet and held her stare. Her heart fluttered. *Oh no!* "Large pizza. Double cheese on my half and loaded with meat on yours—"

"With a side of fries and a root beer." He finished with a grin before he got up to place the order at the long, wooden counter.

In the background, she listened to him joke around with Seth Owens, her friend's shy teenaged brother. Cody had the touch and a way with people, making friends with everyone he encountered.

That was one of the many things she adored about Cody. He made everyone around him feel special and at home.

Maybe that was what was going on with her. His focused attention left her out of sorts. *Yeah, that's it!*

Perhaps Miss Peaches and Miss Clementine had it right. Cody and she shouldn't spend too much time together— alone! It made things awkward and yanked her out of her comfort zone with him.

If she didn't watch it, she'd be on dangerous ground before she knew it.

As if you're not already!

Hannah fiddled with arranging and rearranging the salt, pepper, and glass cheese shaker as she waited. Her jumbled feelings were too disturbing to face. But they nagged at the edges of her mind.

A few days ago, her only problems in the world were how

did she say no to Rodney Ellis, while smoothing over the little blip of him forking over some cash to invest in her business, and get her prized bull selected for the big show. The first was a nuisance to deal with while the second required grit and determination. Two things she had plenty of all her life.

Now, doubts kicked up like a dust storm in the middle of nowhere, twirling around and gaining strength until they whipped her out of her complacency.

She didn't do intense. The few guys she'd dated were from the rodeo circuit. They'd had a mutual understanding. Nothing ever lasted. *Have fun and when there was no more fun to be had, move on. No regrets. No hard feelings.*

Mentally, she brushed her hands. *Done!*

Cody had the same motto. It suited them both.

So why this? Why now?

He came back with her cold, brown bottle of root beer and one for himself. Settling in, he held up his bottle. "Toast."

"And what are we toasting, may I ask?" But she automatically did the same.

"To us." He clinked his against hers before she could protest.

"Us?" Her voice squeaked.

"Our getaway tonight."

She let out a pent-up breath. "I'll drink to that." The combination of the sweet taste and fizzy bubbles made her moan. "So good. When I die can you bury a six pack of this stuff with me?"

"Not the real deal?"

"This, my friend, is better. And who wants to drink piss-warm beer?" She chuckled along with him.

"Not me, for sure." His grin lingered.

Her breath hitched. A beat of silence stretched. *That never happened between them before.*

"You look pretty tonight."

Hannah jerked her head up, meeting his twinkling gaze. Something tugged, hard and sharp, in the deepest part of her chest. "Thanks, Cods." Her words sounded sexy and sultry even though she'd tried to keep it on a friend level by using his nickname.

He shrugged. "I guess I don't say that enough to you."

"Do you say that to your guy friends? I don't think so. Then why would you to me?" *This was getting way out of hand.*

"You're my fee-on-say now." He gave her that ridiculous accent.

"Don't be goofy. It's pretend, remember?"

Cody held up the bottle to his lips. "It doesn't have to be." He tilted it back and took a swig while eyeing her reaction.

"Have you lost your mind? Seriously? You and me?" Her throat closed. "Ah, we don't want to get hitched or have you forgotten?" It came out strangled. "You know, nobody's ever going to live up to what we saw firsthand—your folks, Gramps and Grams. It just doesn't happen like that anymore."

It certainly hadn't with her parents. One-sided, blind devotion did not look good on a woman, especially her sweet, suffering mother. *I'll be damned if history repeats itself with me.*

But Hannah had been enthralled to witness Cody's besotted grandparents all these years. It was rare and touching.

An ache of longing whispered in her heart.

"Yo, Cody!" Seth called out, gaining their attention. "Your order's ready."

He went to get up. "Think about it, Hann. We know what we want—save the ranch for my family and get your bulls in the finals. No distractions if we join forces. I got your back. You got mine. What better way to fend off people like Rodney and Tabitha and whoever else happens to come along?"

"Win-win, right?" But her words sounded wobbly even to her own ears.

Suddenly a pounding on the window rent the air. The glass rattled. They jumped in unison. Jacob banged it again.

His blue eyes were big and he kept looking over his shoulder. "Cody, hurry, man! Film broke. Lights went on. You two are missing in action. Miss Peaches and Miss Clementine are fit to be tied! They're getting a search party together!"

Cody cursed, low and long.

Hannah hustled out of the booth, reached over, and then tugged him along. "Let's go, Cods!"

"Here! Heard Jacob and boxed it up." Seth shoved the hot pizza at Cody.

Her belly growled at the scent of tomato sauce and yummy toppings.

"Thanks!" Cody called as they headed out the big, double wooden and glass doors. They ran down the three stone steps.

"Do not wreck my truck, Cuz!" Jacob backed up as he spoke. "I'll head them off. You owe me. Big time for this one, Cod."

"Got it!"

She grabbed Cody's elbow and dragged him toward the truck a few yards away. "Wait! Give me my truck keys."

He fished in his pocket and found the ring and handed it over. Hannah tossed it to Jacob. They jangled as they sailed through the air. He caught them in his cupped palms.

"Take my truck and park it at the sisters' house. They'll think I went home. Confuse them. And a temporary diversion."

Jacob chuckled. "God, you two are mighty good at this sneaking around stuff." He laughed and then rushed off.

"Just been doing it half our lives, right, Hann?" Cody held open the door for her, none to gingerly lifted her up and in, and then shoved the pizza box at her.

She chuckled as he rounded the truck and then hopped in beside her. "Where to, partner in crime?"

"I got the perfect spot."

His endearing look—mischievous and melting—tugged at her heart. *Yep, you just hit the raw, tender spot, too.*

"Take me away, Cody McCall." She bit her lip, thinking she'd never give permission to anyone else to do that.

She trusted him with her life. Now, could she trust him with her heart?

CODY GLANCED OVER at an ever-increasingly quiet Hannah, trying to gauge her mood. It was never this difficult until now.

It surprised him to realize he didn't like it one bit.

They'd shared everything since growing up—victories, pranks, goofs, stumbles, and gut-wrenching heartaches. Nothing came between them.

Funny how pretending to be engaged had forged a wedge smack dab in the middle of who they were.

Nope, Cody did not like where this was headed.

The thought that beat with each pulse struck home again—do anything possible to save them. He'd lost too much. He sure the hell wasn't going to lose Hannah, too.

He drove down the familiar roads and pointed the truck out of town. He flicked on the high beams, the arch of light spilling long and wide to guide him. The wheels hummed along. The engine purred. And the plush seats absorbed the bumps in the road. *Smooth.*

Not so much them.

Reaching over, he turned the radio knob to Hannah's favorite new country station. The DJ broke in as the last strains of the song faded away.

His chatter eased the tension.

A catchy tune came on, one they'd danced to at The Giddy Up the other night.

"Turn that up, Cods."

He did, smiling when she sang along. Cody joined her and they finally found some harmony. *Yep, they were the life of the party!*

The half-hidden entrance came into sight and he flicked on the left blinker. He turned the steering wheel with ease down the narrow, dusty road.

"To the ridge?"

Glancing over at her, he saw her tucked in the shadows of the cab. *Why did she scoot back more?*

"Alone. At last." Somehow, he had to work things out with her.

This was the best place to do that. The McCall ranch— the long, winding back entrance to the ridge on the land— proved both private and a place he knew they both loved.

Another flicker of doubt arrowed through his gut.

They still had that, didn't they?

Chapter Nine

C ODY MANEUVERED THE truck, twirling the wheel with the heel of his left hand as he backed up. He angled the vehicle perfectly and then parked it in place.

Hannah opened the door and jumped out, pizza box in hand. By the time he'd gotten to her, she'd popped the tailgate down and deposited the box there.

"I'll help you up."

"I got it." She avoided him, clinging to her side and stepping up on the bumper and then hauling herself up.

The glimpse of her bare leg, all the way up her thigh, and nearly to her hip caused his throat to clamp shut. He swallowed hard, once, twice, and still he had a difficult time getting that scratchy sandpaper feeling to end.

He jumped up beside her, shifting the weight of the bed. "Tool box?" He waved to the long, metal tool box running the width of the truck butted up against the cab.

Her boots click clacked as she walked toward it and found a spot. She hissed. "Cold."

"I could hunt for a blanket in the back…"

"Jacob's known for doing lots of things on that. No,

thanks." She chuckled softly.

It sounded like music to his ears. The knot in his belly loosened a little.

Bringing the pizza with him, he settled beside her. "Lukewarm at best. But, it's grub." He lifted the lid.

"I'm starving." She dug in. "Wait, that's yours." She handed it over and nabbed her a slice of extra cheese. Then she proceeded to sink her teeth in and moan. "So good."

They ate in silence for quite some time, gobbling up the tasty pizza, and glancing out over the land.

"Why didn't we bring some beer—root or otherwise?"

"We're on the lam, remember? The pizza bandits?" He tried to make a joke.

It fell flat. Nothing felt the same, especially when he snuck another peek at her lips as she licked them now.

He'd been hard pressed not to watch her mouth move as she chewed. *He'd kissed his Hannah. And he liked it! A hell of a lot!*

He diverted his attention away from her and focused on the surroundings. The fingernail slice of moon seemed to wink down upon them. But the stars—big, bright, and sparkling—dotted the dark blue sky and sucked the air out of his lungs. "Beautiful."

Awe rushed over and through him. The hills and trees spread out before them. In the valley, he heard the cows moo and watched their dark shadows meander to the manmade tank of water at the bottom. The necessity of building this one and two more in prime spots nestled in the property years ago proved life-saving to hundreds of heads of cattle in the long, brutal drought that Texas had endured.

However, it tested the McCalls by seeking out drastic measures and stretching their budget. Grams' illness had brought them to their knees and her passing had shaken them all to their core. Gramps most of all.

"You love this place."

Her words, soft as feathers over his skin, made him shiver. "I'd do anything to save it." *And my family.*

"If you go back on the circuit you'd earn the money to pay off the mortgage." Hannah knew his worries and his secrets.

"That did cross my mind." And he missed her. Gone were the days when they traveled together from one town to the next, hauling their gear and her bulls. Road trips with Hannah were fun and memorable. "You miss my snack addiction, don't you?" He'd pack a sack of treats Grams or Rose baked and, when he ran out, he'd stop and load up again.

"Who knew there were dozens of choices?" Her voice held a smile.

She and he would chip in and buy old favorites and, with every excursion, hunt for a new one to try. That and kick up their boots at honky-tonks and dives, knowing they were there for a good time. No fuss. No muss. No strings attached. Just best friends.

And then there were the times—few and far between—when they talked long into the night as his or her truck thumped along the long, lonely highway, making them imagine they were the only souls left in the world.

They shared their hopes and dreams and fears.

She'd never reveal his nor he would hers. They were sacred. *She* was sacred to him.

"I miss my friend." Hannah's words, whisper-quiet, settled somewhere deep in his heart.

"Here, too." Cody admitted what they'd both been feeling.

"Cods." She swallowed hard enough for him to hear it. Hannah dropped the unfinished piece back in the box, closed the lid, and then placed it on the other side of her. She brushed off her hands and scooted closer. "This isn't us. We're not a couple."

"Just a team." He knew where she headed. *Turning tail at the first sign of a relationship. Again.* Cody rested his elbows on his thighs and hung his head down. A breath stayed trapped in his chest, squeezing tight. "Call it off then."

"Works for me."

"Gramps…he'll be so disappointed." How could Cody do this to the man who meant everything to him?

Hannah placed a hand on his back. Warmth seeped in the cold recesses in his body. A curl of desire flared to life. He stilled.

Her breath caught.

His heart jolted.

"Can we keep pretending?" He couldn't figure out if he asked about the fake engagement or their growing attraction.

"Good time Cody and Hannah. We're the life of the party."

Doubts crept in. Had they always put up a wall between them from not going to that scary place? *A safe, invisible wall to hide behind.*

She tugged her hand away, shook it as if it stung and flexed her fingers.

Cody leaned against the cold metal of the truck cab, tipping his cowboy hat back and looking skyward. "Just think at how small we are and our problems are compared to that."

"Pretty amazing, isn't it?"

"My favorite spot in the world."

"Even after? I mean…how after losing your folks out here. The stampede." She choked out each word.

Somehow, he figured she blinked back stinging tears. There were only two things that would make her do that— talking about losing his folks and the memory of her parents dying. The pulsating emptiness echoed. Rarely, did either one tread there now.

Shared pain and loss bonded them in ways no one else would ever know. "Hann, if you focus on the bitterness you miss the beauty."

Silence fell, comforting and welcome.

Dwelling on the horror of that day only made it worse.

The McCall family deserved better. To honor the fallen, they protected the land and the lifestyle that had taken so much.

She shivered and hugged herself.

"Cold?" Realization kicked in. She sat in a thin dress with skin—beautiful, soft skin—exposed to the chilly night. "Come here." He wrapped an arm around her and tugged her to his side. She fit perfectly, her head tucked between his chin and shoulder and her arm gingerly resting on his chest. Hannah spread out her hand, palm pressed to his thumping heart.

Her breath whooshed out.

Cody shivered and not from the dip in temperature outside.

"Do you think...we can ever get what we had back, Cods?"

He felt the dampness through his shirt. Cody clamped his eyes shut at the thought of her tears. "No, sweetheart. We can't. As much as we want to, we can't go backward. Or erase everything that's happened between us in the last few days."

"I don't want to get married. Not now. Probably never. And me, a mother?" She half chuckled, half choked. "I can barely take care of myself. I live in one room with a teeny tiny attached bath with two spinster sisters as my landlords. I pour every cent I have into my bulls and building my business."

"You're great with kids." He rubbed her cold arm, trying

to warm her and stop her from beating herself up.

"Yeah! Give me a slingshot and spit balls and I'm every kid's friend."

His chuckle shook them and she joined him. "Did you have to teach them to aim so low? Seriously, Hann, you could hurt someone."

"Better that than an eye."

"Butts are fine, but not fronts."

She cringed. "Oops!"

Cody sighed. In this moment, he never wanted to let go of her. Somehow, he knew he had to for both their sakes. "I have to take care of Gramps. And the ranch. My brothers and I will always do that. And I promised Grams."

"Is that what happened with Tabitha? I mean the rush to get hitched and all?"

"Think so. Never wanted to delve deep into that."

Another pause beat between them.

Hannah shifted, pushing away. She disengaged far enough to sit back and look at him. The shadows played over her delicate, heart-shaped features and he couldn't read her eyes in the darkness. But he sensed her full withdrawal from him.

The loss swept over and through Cody. An invisible hand clutched and squeezed his heart.

"We have to tell them the truth, Cods. There's no way we can go through this charade anymore. The faster we do it the faster we get back to our lives."

"And us?" It hurt to ask. Somehow, he knew no matter how much he fought for them, she would build a wall between them, cutting off any possibility of picking up where their friendship had broken off. *Who could ignore the slow, drugging desire after those heated kisses?*

"I'm hoping we can find something…anything to hold us together."

Her unspoken doubts echoed his. "We're not going to, are we?"

A little gasp escaped her parted lips.

"The more we come together, the harder you're pushing away from me. If we admit it—this, us—then how can we ever be just friends again? Awkward turns to uncomfortable, which ends up being avoidance. You and me have that thing in common, you know, don't feel, don't talk about feeling."

"Stop the hurt by any means possible."

Cody couldn't stand it any longer, couldn't release all they had without one last connection. He leaned closer. He reached out and sank his fingers in her silky hair, cupping the back of her head in his hand at the same moment he kissed her.

A hot jolt rushed through him at the touch. *Soft. Luscious.* He moaned. Or was it her? Either way, she pressed into him, seeking and searching. She knocked his hat off. It hit the truck bed with a dull thud.

Hannah's fingertips brushed along his jaw and then his neck, down to the sensitive spot where his pulse pounded away. A shiver coursed through him.

He delved deeper, sliding his tongue along the seam of her lips, parting them. She met his and shoved his shoulders back as she straddled his hips.

She was there, her legs cradling him as he throbbed and now clutched her oh so lush bottom. His head spun. His heart hammered. She took. He gave. His hunger swirled and tightened.

Her soft pleadings reached down. He growled, low and deep.

Shivers racked her. "Cody, I want you."

"God, me, too. You." He gulped in air. His body ached with raw need.

A cow mooed—loud and long—beside the truck. They jumped. Hannah reared back. Cody lunged forward, trying to catch her. But she tumbled to the bed, bringing him with her. They landed with a heavy clatter. Her head thwacked against the metal.

"Hann, you all right?"

She made a choked sound.

"Did I hurt you? Are you crying?" Cody scrambled to his knees, gripping her upper arms as she fought to sit up. He brushed a sweep of her hair away from her eyes.

"Cow chaperones? Really?" Hannah burst out laughing.

Relief shot through him. His heart kicked, hard and swift, at the sweet musical sound. *Damn, McCall, you got it bad!*

"This is still our breakup, right?" Her voice shook.

He couldn't figure out if she was happy or sad about it. Something cold plunged to his gut.

Oh, no, not going there!

Chapter Ten

HANNAH SWIPED A quick look at Cody from under her lashes. Her cheeks burned. *Who would have thought stray calves wandering away and their momma cows would save the day and more embarrassment for her?*

Cody's hands, sure and steady on the steering wheel, directed them back to town.

With each mile, time ticked. At the end of the road, they'd be done.

There was not a place on her that wasn't bruised, especially on the inside. The fall with his heavy weight on top of her might leave marks, but the ones that hurt the most were hidden.

Soon, she'd lose her best friend.

Maybe she had hours or days ago. However, she couldn't quite admit it then. It seemed so much harder to do it now.

All the things she'd heard about his kisses were true. Well, better than she'd heard. *Sin with a six pack!*

Back then, she'd covered her ears and made sounds— hums or noises—to blot out the girls' mighty praises of Cody McCall's highly sought after skills.

Hot? You know it! Desirable? Oh, yeah!

He knew his way around a woman, that was for sure.

Thank goodness she hadn't tempted fate ages ago. At least, she'd had his friendship. *Until now.*

Something hard and crushing clamped down on her heart. She blinked back burning, unshed tears.

If he ever found out what she was thinking or sensing or feeling...

"Flashing lights ahead." He leaned forward, ducking his head to see. "Caleb's on duty tonight." Tension edged his voice.

She swallowed hard, noting the blue and red beams slicing through the darkness as they edged into the outskirts of town. *No, don't let anything happen to anyone else in Cody's family.* He didn't deserve all that hurt. Not when he hadn't even healed from his Grams.

With ease, he steered them down lanes and streets, growing closer.

Clutching the door handle, Hannah's blood ran cold. "That's my place. Miss Peaches? Miss Clementine?" A fresh bout of tears stung.

No! They might be pains at times, but they'd taken her in after her folks died and she lost her home to the bank and they'd put up with her hijinks time and time again.

"No smoke. No fire." Cody slowed down as car after car lined the street and people rushed toward the boarding house.

She reached out, clutching the dash. Her knuckles turned white. "Do you see an ambulance? Mr. Samuels got lightheaded the other night." He'd had a little too much sherry, got up, and then plunked right back down in his chair. The sisters nearly fainted from worry. They were her ragtag family. *Please don't let anything happen to them.*

"Don't see a wagon." He halted, pressing down the window. More people streamed by. He flagged down a couple of cowboys. "Yo, what's going on?"

"Cody, is that you?" Surprise and relief chased across Jackson's face. "Cuz, they were going to send the hounds out after you." He climbed up on the sideboard and peered in. "Hannah, thank God you're all right."

"I'm fine. What's going on?"

"You don't know?" He jerked back and jumped down, raising his hands. "Go see for yourselves." He shook his head and his friend Tyson pointed to the boarding house driveway.

"Some cousin you are," Cody muttered, easing his foot off the brake and letting the truck crawl the last few yards before he signaled to turn in. He beeped the horn—two blasts, short and quick—to get people out of the way.

"What in the world?" Hannah blinked at the flood of lights and the crowd forming. The sisters were clinging to each other and the doors of Hannah's truck were wide open. Caleb used his flashlight to check the interior.

"There's Gramps." Cody bumped along the drive and

pushed the gear to park. He shut down the engine.

Left McCall, holding his shotgun, leaned against the back of Caleb's patrol car. His pet miniature horse stood close by.

Hannah pressed the button and threw off the seatbelt, scrambling to keep up with Cody as he popped open his door. He turned back to help her to the ground.

She clutched his hand as they half ran toward his grandfather.

"Caleb!" Gramps shoved away from the car and meandered to them. "They've been found."

The murmurs of the growing crowd and shuffling of their feet eased. The sheriff—Cody's oldest brother—swung the flashlight around until the beam landed on them.

Hannah and Cody put up their hands to shield their eyes from the brilliant light. Caleb shifted it to their feet, sighing heavily as he strolled to them.

"Mind telling me what's going on?" At over six foot, with a stern look on his face, and with his official badge pinned to the front of his shirt, he appeared daunting to her. *As usual!*

"I was just about to ask you that, brother." Cody turned slightly to his grandfather. "Gramps, what's got you out here with your shotgun and Sweet Potato at your side?"

His Gramps pushed back his cowboy hat until it sat on the back of his head. "Well, son. Miss Peaches and Miss Clementine were distraught." He glanced at Cody and then shifted to take in Hannah. "Your dress is torn at the shoulder. And you both have dirt on your clothes."

"The truck." Hannah gulped. Frowning, she sought the sisters out who were now half walking, half jogging to them. "Distraught?"

"Yeeeppp." Gramps stretched out the one word. "Seems like you went missing, little Hannah. They were accusing Cody of kidnapping you."

"Kidnapping?!" Cody and she cried out in unison.

"Several witnesses stated they saw you, Cody, grab Hannah and force her out of the movie theater and into Jacob's truck." Caleb shook his head, a smirk tugging up the side of his mouth. "Seeing the action adventure flick may have added to the embellishments some."

"For the love of—" Cody halted in mid-curse as Hannah stomped on his foot. "Geez, Hann. That smarts. Again?"

"Oh, my!" Miss Peaches waved her white hanky and then pressed it to her mouth. "You've been defiled, dear."

"De-what?" Cody chuckled. "We went for a drive."

"Alone?" Miss Clementine straightened to her full height of five ten and tilted back her head. "That does it, Cody McCall! You either marry her or I'll put a buckshot in your backside the likes you'll never forget. And I'll make sure no one in this town ever does business with you again. Is that clear?"

Gulping, Hannah clung to Cody's hand. Miss Clementine would use her mighty resources and try. Oil money spoke volumes. Whether she succeeded or not, only time would tell. However, the damage would linger for Cody and all of the McCalls.

"Can't say as I blame her, son." Gramps grimaced. "You're toying with Miss Hannah's reputation now."

"You're already engaged, so what's stopping you?" Caleb cocked an eyebrow at his brother.

Hannah froze, feeling cornered. Growing up, Caleb could always tell when they'd been up to no good. Why should this time be any different?

She gazed around at the townspeople, taking them in and the concern written all over their features. All of them had worried about her safety. How could she let them down now? How could she jeopardize Cody and his future if she backed out now?

It could ruin him!

Going from pretend engagement to admitting their friendship as they had known it was over only a short time ago rocked her to her core. Her world without Cody would never be the same. *Hollow. Empty.*

It was for their own good. *Wasn't it?* She'd save them both from that marriage and divorce runaround that her parents had thrived on. She'd saved him from her demons of never living up to what he wanted and needed in a wife.

But, at this critical second in time, doing what was just and right for Cody—her very best friend in the whole entire world—dragged her to her senses.

Squeezing Cody's hand, she prayed she did the right thing. The cool night air grew heavy. Silence stretched. You could have heard a pin drop among the fifty or more people surrounding them.

"Well, who doesn't love a good country wedding, right, Cods?" She turned to him.

His eyes were filled with uncertainty and a hint of panic, most likely the same way hers were at the moment. The strain around his tight lips stood out. Visions of his close call last year flashed in her mind. Jealousy had sat heavy on her chest for months, watching the couple. *No, watching Cody be dragged away from her by another woman.*

Hannah finally admitted how she never wanted to lose him. Ever. To anyone else. Even if she wasn't there to witness it. *But marriage to her best friend?* It was difficult to suck in a breath as the swirling, out-of-control sensation gripped her hard.

We make a good team. Then. Now. Hopefully in the future. A bubble of panic rose, nearly choking her. She cleared her throat. "So, Cody McCall, you want to marry me? Sooner rather than later, that is?" She tacked on the last for his family, the sisters, and the townspeople leaning forward and hanging on the edge of her words.

"Hannah…" Cody swept her with a lingering gaze. The grim look altered slightly. A curious light shone in his eyes. "You ready to be my rebellious bride?"

THE STILLNESS SETTLED on his shoulders the second Cody entered the back entrance to the big ranch house. He wiped his boots on the mat in the mud room and crossed over the threshold in to the darkened kitchen. Ever since his Grams died last year this room didn't feel the same. *Nothing felt the same!*

The light from Gramps' office down the hall beckoned. His grandfather waited up for him. *Could he face Gramps tonight? Hell,* he *didn't even know where he stood with Hannah. She'd never answered his question.*

Leaving Hannah safe and sound in her little rented room at the sisters' house over an hour ago left a hollow feeling in his chest.

What a fiasco!

Thankfully, Caleb had shooed the curious onlookers away, sent Gramps home, instructed Miss Peaches and Miss Clementine to remain calm while returning to their house, and sent Cody and Hannah to hash things out.

Only talking didn't come. Heavy, pulsing silence sat between them like a cold iron anvil and hammer.

Fear flooded Hannah's beautiful brown eyes. His chest clutched.

"I thought…we could fake this…thing." Her stuttering words echoed in his mind. "There're so many people…involved." Guilt washed over her features. "Pretend.

Then end it."

At first, that was his plan, too. He sighed. The more connected they were the more he liked the idea of marrying her. He needed her in his life. But did she need him or this? "My question still stands, Hannah." He dropped a kiss on her forehead and left her there staring after him.

Now, Cody drew near the office.

"'Bout time, son." Gramps leaned his head against the back of his favorite leather chair with his feet on the matching ottoman.

Cody glanced at the large empty area nearby where his grandmother's hospital bed had stood the last weeks of her life. Something tugged, hard and sharp.

She'd wanted to be close to the family pictures and books lined up on the floor-to-ceiling shelves. Through the years, she'd read every single one and some more than once. For a woman who had to drop out of high school to help support her family by working as a cowgirl, she'd done her darnedest to educate herself. His grandmother had done that, wed Gramps, and raised her son, and then her grandsons. The McCall family would be nothing without her love and guidance.

"You gonna step in or not?"

"Can't get away with much around here, can I?" He entered slowly, still swept away in memories of those long, sad days of watching her wither away.

Sweet Potato lifted his head from the pile of quilts he

slept on near Gramps' chair. Occasionally, the horse would allow his grandfather to pet him.

"About tonight—"

"Never you mind that." He shifted his legs. "Sit."

The order prompted Cody to obey without comment. He plopped down on the ottoman, preparing himself. *Let's get this over.* "Shoot."

"Did I ever tell you about my wedding day?"

Thinking back, he couldn't recollect that one. "No, sir."

He opened one eye and peeked at Cody. "I bolted."

"What! You?" Surprise lanced through him.

Gramps' looked at him fully now. "Yep. I was all nervous and twitchy waiting on your Grams." He waved his hand. "It could have had something to do with being in a church, too—back then I stayed far away from the house of worship. But, when I spotted her coming down the aisle she looked like an angel. And I knew this devil could never settle down, so I turned tail. Right to The Giddy Up."

Cody had never heard this before. He frowned. "What did Grams do?" He couldn't imagine what she'd thought or how she reacted.

"I barely had my first shot down before she stormed in after me and unleashed that good verbal beat down she gave when she got all riled up, remember?" He chuckled and shock his head. "Curses and all. That's when I looked at her and knew I'd regret it every day of my life if I let her go."

His throat closed. *That's how I feel about Hannah.*

"She turned me down flat."

"But...she must have said yes."

"I didn't give her a choice to take me back. Nope, she was still giving me hell, especially after I picked her up and slung her over my shoulder. She hit me on the back all the way out the door and down the sidewalk back to the church."

Laughing at the image he painted, Cody shook his head. "And then she said yes?"

"Nah. I had to kiss her over and over again right there in from of the preacher and guests. I must have worn her down at some point, 'cause she finally threw up her hands and kissed me back."

"Ah, Grams. She could never resist you, Gramps."

"Good times, son." He choked up. "She had her heart set on you and little Hannah ending up together."

Cody stilled. "She never said..."

"To me, she did. Even back in the day when you were kids, she'd say, 'wouldn't it be something if our Cody and Hannie grew up, fell in love, got married, and gave us some great-grandbabies?'"

Yeah, wouldn't it?

Gramps reached over on the table beside him, grabbed something, and thrust it at Cody. "Your Grams' ring. She'd want you to have it. She always had a soft spot for you, son. Probably from the day you were born, but especially since you were there that day and saw your mama and daddy…Well, you know."

The stampede. His heart clutched. Flashes of cattle racing, dust swirling, sounds of their distress, and the ground shaking rushed back as if it were yesterday. His father had thrown himself over Cody's mother to protect her. They'd found them holding hands, quiet and still.

"Take it. Hopefully it got some of what we had and will give it to you two."

The weight of it sat in his palm—not just the shiny, gold ring, but the legacy.

Could Hannah and he do this? For themselves and his family?

Chapter Eleven

"I GOT YOU on speaker phone, but you're fading in and out. I could lose you at any time. Now, what's this all about?" Hannah spun the steering wheel and headed down the road to the McCall ranch. The familiar lane, fields, and trees brought an ache to her chest. She loved this place.

Sandy's voice mingled and overlapped with Julie's and they nearly shouted. "A dress, for God's sake! You need a wedding dress. You can't get married in jeans, girl!"

She swallowed hard. Her mother wouldn't be there. Then again, maybe she wouldn't, either.

"Miss Peaches said…" Static crackled.

"Say again."

The line died.

Great! Once Miss Peaches and Miss Clementine heard they'd never leave it alone. *A proper wedding!*

Slowing, she entered under the big wooden arch and sign *The McCall Ranch.* Her heart swelled with love and pride for the land she'd grown up on. At six years old, when her daddy was laid up with a broken arm from being thrown off a bull on the rodeo circuit, her parents and she had lived in one of the crew's houses here. It had been the happiest time of her life.

Cody and her. Thick as thieves. Then. But what about a future?

Hannah spotted Gramps in his camouflage utility vehicle, waiting near the house. She frowned and pulled alongside of him. Sweet Potato sat in the back, chewing on a bouquet of fresh flowers. "Everything all right?"

"Fine and dandy."

"Waiting on someone?"

"You."

"Me?"

He waved a hand for her to park. "Hurry up, Hannie. It's not like we've got all day."

She chuckled, gave him a jaunty salute, and then did as he said. Few people argued with Left McCall these days. Hannah frowned at the empty space where Cody usually parked his black truck. She joined Gramps. "Where's Cody? His truck's not here."

"Didn't he tell you?" The older man eyed her. "Sold it."

"But...why?"

Gramps sighed. It came out heavy and strained. "He paid some back taxes."

On the ranch. So, that's how he'd come up with the money. He'd shrugged it off a few weeks ago when they talked on the phone. However, she'd just assumed he had leftover rodeo money. She fought back a well of tears. *God, she couldn't be more proud of her Cody.*

She held on for dear life as Gramps put the peddle to the metal. They bounced over the long, dirt driveway, the extended yard, and down the path.

"I'm supposed to meet Cody." She pointed a thumb in the opposite direction and toward the barn. "Where are you taking—" She couldn't finish.

"Like you don't know." He tsked. "Hang on, Sweet Potato. And stop eating my flowers."

Something strangled her chest, tightening. *No, not there!*

The vehicle rattled over the well-worn track.

Gramps hollered over the noise.

She didn't hear a word; her ears pounded.

In moments, he drew to a halt. "You can look now. It ain't gonna bite you, Hannie."

The old family cemetery sat there under a nest of huge oak trees.

"Come on, you can't hide forever." Gramps reached back and grabbed the bouquet. "Worse for wear, Tater. You'd think I didn't feed you the way you've munched up all the petals. And just look at the slobber." He sighed, getting out and then strolling to the newest, charcoal gray stone yards away. He removed his cowboy hat at Wilhelmina McCall's gravesite. "Hey, honey bunch, look who decided to visit today."

"Dragged, is more like it." Hannah grudgingly hefted herself out of the tiny farm vehicle.

Gramps gazed down and talked to his beloved, deceased wife. "Prettiest cowgirl I ever saw, you were. I still remember you in your favorite pink and blue plaid shirt, pink scarf, big buckle—McCall ranch buckle, I stand corrected—your blue jeans, and your dancing cowgirl boots, matching hat in your hand."

Hannah eased back a step, wondering if she could slip away and not intrude upon his time.

"Where you going, little lady?"

"Um…" *Did he have eyes in the back of his head now?*

"Hold your horses." He chuckled. "You always turned tail at the mushy stuff. That's after you rolled your eyes. Don't you think we didn't notice? Yep, your daddy fed your momma lots of lines, so I can see why you're a little shy."

"Do we have to discuss this here?"

"Winnie doesn't mind. In fact, she likes to put her two cents in. Always did."

"Ah, Gramps, you hearing voices?" Over the last few months, Cody and she wondered if his eccentric ways were a little more than just that. Hannah gulped hard. No one had taken Grams passing harder than him, but still…talking to her, treating Sweet Potato like a pet dog, and today with this? He had perked up a bit since the engagement, though.

He seemed to direct the next to Hannah. "One of the best and brightest, my Winnie. I'd have nothing if it weren't for her. We built the ranch from scratch, long days and long nights tending to the cattle and calves without mommas. A cowboy needs a strong cowgirl by his side."

And there you have it! What better way to get Cody and her down the aisle faster than to make her feel guilty as all get out? Pushy, pushy, pushy!

"I aim on winning this one, Hannie."

She groaned. "And I thought you liked me, too."

THE BRAKES SQUEAKED as Gramps came to a halt yards away from all the activity nearby. "Here you go, little lady." His voice held a grin.

But all Hannah could do was stare at Cody McCall in the second story opening of the faded red barn, hauling hay bales from the rafters, fitting the metal hook on the end of the pulley under the rope that held the bale together, and then easing it down into the bed of the old, rusty ranch truck resting beneath.

Brilliant afternoon sunlight beat down on Cody's shirt-less torso. His slick skin glistened. His shoulders and biceps bunched and flexed as he heaved another bale of hay in position and then lowered it down.

Hannah gulped. A low, steady hum went off in her body. Slowly, she got out of the vehicle and watched.

One of the ranch hands, Mateo, in the bed of the truck made short work of unclipping it and piling it on top of the others.

Cody swiped the back of his gloved hand across his sweaty brow. His shrill whistle and two bangs on the side of the barn caught his friend's attention from the cab of the truck. "Yo, Johnny, haul it!"

"I'm Juan, remember?" He chuckled, sticking his head out the driver's side window and then glanced up at him.

"Not you, too?"

"Hey, if the big guy wants to call me Shirley next, I'm good with that." Johnny slash Juan gave a wave before he took off down the path with Mateo nestled in the bays and hanging on.

"Don't you think your wife would have a problem with that one?!" Cody shouted after him.

She chuckled. His grandfather had them all wrapped around his little finger, including her. Standing there, she watched the tires kick up dirt and dust. She turned back to realize Cody stared at her.

Pinpricks of awareness chased down her spine. Heat began a slow burn in her middle and spread.

"Now, kids, here's your picnic lunch Rosa fixed for you." Gramps grunted as he got out of the cart and hauled out the hidden basket beneath the red and black checked wool blanket. "Don't tell her, but I snuck a couple of bottles of her favorite orange soda pop in there, too." Coming up beside her, Gramps shoved the basket at Hannah. She caught the handles and hefted the weight of it. "Go on. It ain't the prettiest or the fanciest, but it'll do." He shot her a glance and then his grandson and nodded curtly.

"You coming up?" Cody dared her.

In the back of her mind, she heard Gramps' booted footsteps walk away and then him climbing back in to his trusty vehicle. It creaked in protest. The motor puttered and soon faded in the distance as he drove away.

Cody placed his hands on his hips, waiting.

Hannah swallowed hard. She never backed away from a challenge and she wasn't about to start now. Her first steps forward were hesitant.

"I'll meet you at the ladder."

"Seriously?" She made a noise in the back of her throat. "You want me, you're going to work for it, Cods." Her double meaning shot out without a filter.

Good thing he laughed.

She marched to the spot under the hook and rope. "Lower it, cowboy."

His sexy grin fueled sparks of warmth from her head to her toes.

Once the large hook rested on the ground, she reached out with one hand to grab the thick rope, stepped in the metal curve with one booted foot, rested the other one on top of the first, and then secured the heavy basket in the crook of her arm. She hung on with both hands. "Your turn!"

Cody tugged her up slow and steady.

As the ground fell away, her cares seemed to do the same.

She swung slightly and her view switched to the ranch, revealing more and more as she ascended. The horses in the corral continued to feed in the trough, the green grass smelled sweet after the quick shower through the night, the cows grazed there and far beyond over the hills, and the trees in the distance sheltered them on the beloved McCall ranch. Her heart tugged.

The breeze caressed her hair and tickled her skin as she shifted again. Now, she gazed up, watching him with that big smile on his face.

"Is this what you call hauling ass?"

She burst out laughing and instantly clung tighter to the scratchy rope. "Technically? Yep!"

Finally, she sat parallel to the opening, coming face-to-face with him. He cocked an eyebrow at her. "Well, hello, Hannah Prescott. It's so good of you to drop in like this."

"Ah, Cods, let's not use the drop word, okay?"

They chuckled in unison.

Wrapping the rope around his back and waist, he planted his feet for leverage. "Hand over the picnic basket, lady."

"Is this a hold up, Yogi?"

"Hann, you're killing me. Don't make me laugh or I might really drop you."

Gingerly, she worked the crushing weight of the basket down her forearm and to her wrist and held it out for him. "Grab it!" Her arm shook with the heavy wicker and contents.

He did, lifting it and relieving her of the burden. "Geez, what did Rose pack, anyway? Half the fridge?" In calculated degrees, and still watching her like a hawk, he eased the basket to the barn floor. "One down. You're next. Ready?"

"As much as I like the picturesque landscape, including man candy, yes." *Oops! She let that slip about him.*

"So, you like?"

"Let's not talk. Action. As in, pull me in already."

"Bossy." But he did reach out, first grabbing the rope below her hands and then yanking it. When it swung toward him, he moved so fast, wrapping his arm around her waist and hauling her in to his body. "Put your arms around my shoulders."

It sounded even more intimate than her body pressed along his at the moment. His was smooth muscles and hard angles and she wanted so much more.

"Trust me." His whispered words went beyond the situation at hand.

Could she? Hannah wrapped first one arm around his bare shoulder, shoved aside the rope, and then clung to him with both arms, kicking out of the hook.

He wrestled her away and released the rope, the metal hook banged against the wooden floor, landing heavily.

Hannah shook.

Cody gripped her tighter to him with her feet still off the ground.

In all their years together, never had she been this close,

his hot skin penetrating the thin layer of her shirt and bra. *No, searing heat!*

His heavy breathing whisked by her ear as he rubbed his cheek against her hair. "You smell like sunshine and flowers all rolled into one."

"And you." She pressed her lips along his collarbone, feeling the shiver rack his body. "You are all male and musk with a hint of hay."

He tried to laugh, but it came out on a puff of air. "Hann…God, I should let you go."

Somehow it came out as a double meaning.

She eased away. "You can let me down now."

Cody blew out a hot breath and slowly let her slide down his chest until her boots hit the floor with a dull thud.

Hannah planted her hands against his flesh, intending to shove away. However, she sucked in air, sharp and quick, at the electricity singeing her palms. Heat flared and her middle tightened in a coil of delicious desire.

"You're trembling."

"Ha, and here I thought that was you." Words tumbled out of her parched lips. She licked them.

He groaned. "Did you have to do that?"

Again she gulped hard. Shaking, she moved away, regretting the loss of his touch as his hands fell away.

Hannah went to the nearby basket. "Lunch. Food. That will help the lightheadedness. As for the shaking…" *And the wobbles. But not the achy feeling. Nope. That seemed to rear up every dang time she saw him now.*

"You're talking to yourself." He moved to secure the rope and hook to the outside of the barn on the left.

She flipped open the basket and snuck a peek at his broad shoulders and down to his lean hips where his jeans sat. A whoosh of heat flared again. *Down, girl!*

In minutes, they sat with their legs dangling out of the barn opening and the food spread out between them.

"Brisket." He moaned as he ate. "Beautiful, isn't it?"

Jerking her head up first to glance at him, she then followed his stare out over the ranch. "Perfect view from up here."

"I love this place, Hann. It's a part of me and I'm a part of it. I'll do anything to save it." He glimpsed at the stone ranch house past his grandmother's gardens in the distance. "For Gramps. For my family. And for me."

"Never a doubt about that. Or that you can." Struggle, going against the odds, were strong suits of Cody's.

"Do this with me. I mean. Let's make this marriage real."

A wave of shock rolled over her. Her need to stay safe and secure pulsed to life. "I don't know… We can fool some of the people some of the time, but *all* the people *all* of the time?"

"I get it. You're scared. Your dad didn't have the best track record."

"You think? My mom adored him and forgave him time and time again. I can't live like that, Cods. You know that."

"Did I ask you to? I'm not the cheating kind, Hann. And you know that. Yeah, I like to have a good time drinking and dancing, maybe a little flirting—if I'm single. But I'm true blue as they come. To you."

A knot formed in her throat. "What about Tabitha? You were ready to marry her last year?"

"Oh, yeah, didn't you know? It's in the past."

"Is it?" She'd wondered if the rodeo queen ever came walking back would he give her a second chance. After all, she dumped him and she'd made certain she let everyone know. *Not the other way around.*

"History. She wants the glory."

Hannah had spotted that a mile away, but how did she get her besotted best friend to acknowledge and accept that? Would his heart always belong to someone else?

She hitched up her leg and with her heel shoved away from the space. With her hands, she maneuvered herself where she leaned her back against the barn framing the opening. Hannah watched as he did the same and soon he sat facing her. He stretched out his long legs, crossing them at the ankles.

"Rodney?"

"Not my type."

"Oh, yeah, he's the marrying kind. You're not."

"So, why don't you believe it?" It was strange talking to him like this. A flicker of intimacy teased her and she longed for more. His features were shuttered, but his eyes searched hers.

"You lie, Hannah Banana." The side of his mouth tilted upward.

Something warm unfurled in her belly. *God, danger should be his middle name. Oh, along with hot and sexy!*

"You want it."

She swallowed. *You? Oh, yeah!*

"But you want guarantees. There are none."

Her heart sank.

Cody must have seen the crushing blow chase across her face; he moved fast and sure, dodging the food and then sat before her. He tugged on her calves until she scooted closer, loosely placing her legs over his thighs. His hands, big and strong, settled on her waist and tugged her a tad closer.

Looking into his green eyes, her world tilted and she tumbled over and over again. "Cods?"

"Yeah. It's me. I'm asking you to trust me. To trust us."

"What if someone…better comes along?"

"Same could be asked about you."

"Ha! Me?"

"Someday, Hannah Prescott, you're going to fall so far and so deep you won't know what hit you. I hope that it's with me."

She shook her head, wondering why she'd gotten all dreamy at his words.

"And our babies."

Her heart hitched clear up to her throat. An ache inside

her grew.

"Yeah, Hann, you. I'd love to see you holding and rocking our baby with all that love you got bottled up. One or a dozen."

"Cody, you can't be serious?" *Them settled down? This was still supposed to be pretend, wasn't it?*

That slow grin of his spread, yanking at places inside her she didn't even know existed.

His eyes lit up. "Give me fifty years and I'll show you."

Chapter Twelve

HANNAH SAT WITH a pasted on smile, listening to dear ol' Mr. Jefferson Samuels go on and on about his historical research today. As the only other boarder at the present, they were both required to attend the fancy, sit-down dinner every night they were home.

He had his distant cousins' rapt attention. Most nights, he did entertain. However, tonight she wished she knew the art of keeping her eyes open while sleeping.

Why did I forget the long yarns he loved to tell? If she had, she'd have made other plans with her girlfriends. But that would lead to questions she didn't want to answer just yet. Like when they would go shopping for her wedding dress and surely the wedding night...

Visions of sexy, handsome Cody popped into her head. She moaned inwardly at the heady distraction.

She'd seen him in the barn dozens of times in the past, so why see him differently now? Why focus on the way his muscles rippled and the sunlight dabbled along his chest making it look bigger and broader this time?

The memory of his gorgeous, green eyes, hooded and

filled with promise, sent a shiver through her now. Why notice him as a sexy, breathtaking cowboy when all he'd ever been was her best friend?

Because things had changed between them in such a short time. *Too many. Too fast.*

Hannah's reeling mind couldn't go there. Not again. A throbbing headache began the moment she'd left the McCall ranch this afternoon. It hammered away whenever she tried to process Cody's urgent requests. *Fifty years?*

They weren't his Gramps and Grams by any stretch of the imagination. No one could be like them, in Hannah's opinion. What they had was rare and unique. *Friendship, love, never raised their voices, and their world revolved around the other.*

"Oh, dear! I forgot the biscuits." Miss Clementine rose from the elegant dining table, bowed slightly, and then half walked, half rushed to the kitchen.

"Slow down, honey. You're bound to break something with those heels you're wearing." Miss Peaches smiled and batted her eyelashes, the edge of her left fake one disengaged from her lid and it had a mind of its own now.

Yep, there it goes again. Up. Blink. Up higher.

"Peaches, won't you help me, sister?" Miss Clementine poked her head around the corner and waved her to go with her.

"Don't be silly. Who will be the host to our lovely guests?" Her blinking picked up speed, seemingly fighting to get the wayward lash back in place.

Nope. Not going back.

The pseudo caterpillar had a mind of its own. It became unglued and began to dangle on the side of her temple. Another furious round of blinking and it dropped into her mashed potatoes.

Hannah suppressed a chuckle and then another one as she turned away from the most ineloquent image. Poor Miss Peaches turned a rather bright shade of pink.

"Oh, my!" She glanced at Mr. Samuels who remained completely wrapped up in his tale of how Texas battled to become a state. With her dessert spoon, Miss Peaches delicately fished out the lash, excused herself profusely, and then rushed to the kitchen.

"I told you not to wear those things." Miss Clementine's stern voice carried.

"I've always wanted to try them. Now, help me clean and reattach this one, sister."

"What?" Mr. Samuels coughed, seemingly coming out of his history fog to return to the present day. "Where are the sisters?" His gray brows dipped low between his brows when he found their empty seats.

"Kitchen mishap." Hannah struggled to keep her lips from twitching.

He appeared lost for a moment. Her heart squeezed for the brilliant man who had only been with them through the winter, wrapped in warm clothes to starve off the constant chill to his arthritic bones. With his gray hair and thick mustache and his preference for three-piece suits even in the south, he reminded her of an absentminded Mark Twain at times.

"Great history." She shot him a tight smile and dug into her food.

The sooner she'd be done the sooner she'd escape to her room and pack an overnight bag. Cody and she would head out at the crack of dawn to check on her bulls and audition Macho for the next rodeo in the long line of getting the bull to the big show.

Cody! She'd be all alone with him for hours on the road trip tomorrow, in connecting rooms when they bunked down… Hannah couldn't get her mashed potatoes down her suddenly clogged throat, never mind her favorite meatloaf.

"Marriage can be a blessing or a curse." His words dropped into the silent air, startling her.

"Why, Mr. Jefferson Samuels, are you speaking from experience?" *A curse?*

"Observation, my dear. After all, I'm a historian. I research. I observe."

"Then come to a conclusion, right?" She sipped from her water goblet.

"It's what the two people in the relationship make of it."

"Attitude?" *What did he know? He'd been single his entire life.*

"Partly. It's the glass half full or half empty philosophy.

It's how you get through things in life—does it beat you down or build you up? Hope."

Hannah gulped down more water and nearly choked. "Advice? Is that it?"

"Did you think I wouldn't?" His mustache twitched and his small, blue eyes twinkled.

"Oh, and I used to like you, too."

His hearty chuckle eased her jangled nerves.

The noises from the kitchen—the oven door closing, a pan set down, and Miss Peaches muttering about the eyelash—continued, but the sisters could barge in at any time. "Before they come back, just give it to me. Good. Bad. Ugly. Have at it."

"That's telling." He took his time raising his delicate tea cup and then drinking from it. He smacked his lips. "Very telling."

"Well, mind telling me?" Now he had her curious.

"It doesn't matter if on the surface you get along or not, for the most part. Some squabbles can be invigorating. Bitter arguments destroying. It's underneath. Are your beliefs similar, your values, morals, even your character? That's the core you stay true to, so that doesn't change. That's who you connect to and fall in love with. Deep down."

"Like if they're selfish or selfless in hard times? If they stay around and weather the storm with you or take off—oh, they're there physically, but not emotionally..." A lump formed and stuck.

She couldn't finish. It scraped on that wound she'd carried with her. Her father—loving and kind to her most times—did not harbor the same ideals as her mother. *Polar opposites.*

Family did not come first with dear ol' daddy. His wants and needs took precedence. They'd struggle for food, keeping the debt collectors at bay, and nearly losing the family home to finance his dreams of first bull riding and then stock contracting, getting the one prize bull for a big payout.

She couldn't do that to a husband and kids, not like her dad had done to her mom and her.

Cody deserved better...

HANNAH TOSSED AND turned, punching her pillow far too many times. She pictured the blush-colored fabric bursting and feathers flying everywhere.

With a heavy heart, she realized she was not the best choice for her best friend. He needed a partner in saving the McCall ranch. She had other ideas of growing her business, just now taking off after seven long years of blood, sweat, tears, and the loan from Cody.

She must have dozed; a tap tapping on her window roused her just before dawn. Coming wide awake, she heard it again.

Shoving off her covers and rolling out of bed, Hannah easily found and grabbed her shotgun propped against the wall nearby. The familiar cold metal fit in her grasp. With her back to the wall, she eased her way around the lone cream-colored armchair and toward the window.

The sound came again. Then a bang against the outside planks followed. Cussing sliced the air.

Hannah breathed a sigh of relief. "Cods." The loud tab had her hustling to the window and throwing it open. "What do you think you're doing? It's not even dawn yet."

"Good to see you, too, Hann." He chuckled softly. "Is that any way to greet your intended?"

"Cods, you'll wake the sisters. Shoo!"

He pressed forward, so she could see his smiling face. That mischievous twinkle in his eyes sent her heart tripping over itself and her middle dipping.

"I'm breaking you out, Hann. You think your self-appointed chaperones will let you go on your own, never mind when they find out I'm going, too?"

She sighed. "You win."

"I know. Now come on. I already picked up your trailer with the bulls."

"What? You stole my truck?"

"Borrowed, Hann."

"How?"

"I'll explain later. Shake a leg, darling."

She groaned at his thick, charming accent. "Stay." There

was no way he could be caught in her bedroom again. Gingerly, she handed him the shotgun.

"Whoa!"

"Protection."

"Ah, and here I thought going to the drug store and picking up a few packs would be protection enough."

"Smart ass!" But she laughed, shook her head, and then jumped into action.

In less than fifteen minutes, she'd thrown off her short nightie, showered, washed her hair, and changed. Going to the window, she hauled her overnight bag. "Psst! You still there?"

"Where else would I be?"

Hannah tossed it through.

A muffled curse word shot back. "You could warn a guy, Hann."

She cringed. "Oops. Sorry. In a rush." Now, she tugged on her boots, hopping to keep upright. She made it to the nightstand and snagged her keys, ID, money, and her cell phone that worked only when it felt like it lately.

"That damn dog again! He's barking."

"No. He can't ruin this, too." She rushed to the window, halted abruptly, and glanced over her shoulder to her door.

"Come on! We'll be found out any minute."

And have to face the sisters! They'd never let her leave without them if they did. Hannah spotted the high back vanity chair. She raced to it, grabbed it, and then, in a few more steps, she wedged the back under the door knob. "That will buy us some time to get out of Dodge!"

Vague noises from above—like feet hitting the floor and shuffling slippers—reached her.

Hannah sprinted to freedom, sticking her head and arms out first. She nearly dove through, but got stuck half in and half out. "Cods. Help!"

His warm chuckle wrapped around and through her.

Not now! Ugh!

He yanked her the rest of the way and she tumbled down, landing on top of him. He grunted. "Damn, girl, we gotta stop meeting this way."

Her pent-up panic bubbled up. Hannah giggled and couldn't stop.

"Shhh!" He rolled them over. His laughter faded away. For a moment, he grew sober, looking down at her upturned face.

Air stayed trapped in her lungs. Everything pulsed inside her, like a heavy drum beat, waiting for more. Cody leaned down inch by agonizingly slow inch. Anticipation danced in her veins. His lips, warm and firm, brushed hers.

She gasped.

He moaned. Cody dipped his head again, but lingered when he kissed her, his lips clinging to hers.

Or was that hers drinking his in? Either way, Hannah melted into a puddle of mush. She had no limbs, no resistance—even if she wanted to resist, which she didn't—just sweet, utter acquiescence to the delicious taste and heat of him.

Cody pulled away first. "Did you hear that?" He stilled as they both listened. A door squeaked closed. "The sisters?" They stayed frozen, waiting.

Panic grabbed her by the throat. She shoved at him. He complied, lifting her by the hand and then helped Hannah gain her feet. She bent to get her bag at the same time he did. They bumped heads.

"Oh, fudge!" She hissed, touching the sore, tender spot on the top of her forehead.

His cuss was far worse than hers.

She giggled again. "Your Grams would wash your mouth out for that one."

"That she would, Hannah Banana."

In moments, their arms were loaded with her bag and shotgun as they snuck around the house.

"Coast is clear."

Hannah followed Cody racing toward the street where her truck with the covered bull trailer stood. "You loaded him for me?"

"All set to go. Caleb helped. He's always good for a covert operation. You know, that military background of his." They reached the side of the vehicle.

She went to her bull, reaching in and stroking his side as he dozed. "Good, boy." Without thought, she jumped in the passenger side. "Thanks, Cody."

He climbed in behind the wheel and turned the ignition. "Don't thank me now. Wait until we escape completely." His nod to the house revealed the light in the second story window flickering on.

"Go. Hurry!"

Hannah figured the moment she let out her first real breath was the exact second when they crossed county lines.

In all the jitters of being caught, she'd brushed aside how her body pressed into his and that slow, deliberate kiss. *And the tingles.*

No one watched. No witnesses. It was only them. Just like in the truck bed. And that scared her.

This wasn't normal for them.

They joked about other couples being oblivious to everything but themselves.

Going down that slippery slope head first without a safety net! Fear and excitement mingled in the pit of her stomach.

No, going off a cliff!

Was there a way to put the brakes on this crazy, wonderful joyride?

Could they ever get back what the always had?

Chapter Thirteen

CODY SENSED HER misgivings; they thickened the air in the cab of the truck as the tires ate up the miles.

His doubts disappeared the moment Hannah and he had looked out over the ranch yesterday. She loved it as much as he did. Sitting there, with her by his side, he'd known there would never be another woman for him. It felt so pure, so right. *His Hannah as his wife.*

That hadn't happened when he'd nearly bought Tabitha her ring—an expensive square-cut one with smaller diamonds around it—she'd all but picked it out for herself by leaving torn out magazine pictures in his truck or tucked in his saddle bag. That brought him up short. The nagging questions. The overwhelming sensation of being suffocated.

For months, the invisible hands around his throat, strangling him, persisted. The hold tightened, cutting off air. With every introduction as his girlfriend, along with the high-anticipated rapid-fire questions of when the big day was, all the unspoken expectations of keeping her in the fancy lifestyle she'd been accustomed to, Cody felt backed into a corner like a caged animal.

Thank goodness, he'd held off proposing to her!

Now, he glanced over at an unusually quiet Hannah gazing out the open window as fields and cattle rushed by in the beginnings of dawn yawning across the horizon. A grin tugged at the corner of his mouth.

He didn't feel those pressing sensations with Hannah. Maybe even the exact opposite...

"Snacks behind me." He pointed a thumb over his shoulder to his loot.

She jerked around quickly, a small smile playing on her slightly swollen pink lips. His gut clutched. He'd drunk there and was thirsty for more.

Hannah unclicked her seatbelt and then shifted to kneel on the seat near his hip. "What did you bring me?"

His chuckle rumbled through his chest. "You are so easy, you know that, Hann? Give you some sweets and you're all over me."

Her nudge on his upper arm seemed like old times, only he sensed her sudden quiver and heard her swallow hard.

"Chocolate soothes the savage beast, right?" She dug in the brown paper sack. "Oh, my God! Muffins!"

"Thank Rose for them. Extra chocolate chips, too."

She moaned. "I've died and gone to heaven."

"Don't forget to share. You know, we'll be doing that a lot in the future."

A deafening silence roared to life between them. Only the tires humming along on the asphalt road echoed.

She slunk back to her side. "Did you have to remind me?"

Cody gripped the steering wheel, his knuckles turning white. "Seems like I do, as a matter of fact."

"Why can't we just be friends, Cods?" The strum of emotion in her voice breathed to life.

"We talked about this, remember?"

"Oh, yeah. That dang truck bed again."

"Won't do any more, Hann." He delivered it gently. "We can do this. Hell, we've been through worse."

Thankfully, she chuckled along with him. "That's just it. If we end it now, we get off easy, well, easier. No added pain and suffering compounded over time." She gulped hard. "We're crossing boundaries. Maybe stepping on toes here." She shot him a sideway glance. "Maybe severing our lifeline."

"You'll be out from under Miss Peaches and Miss Clementine's thumb. No more curfew or penance for something they thought you did."

"They've always been good to me, taking me in when my folks…the accident happened and I lost the house. In some ways, they're family. Even Mr. Samuels."

"Can't disagree with that. Gramps and Grams wanted to take you in."

"They told me as much."

"You said no." At the time, it had hurt. It was difficult being rejected by someone who'd always seemed like a part of him. Glancing at her, he watched the play of emotions chase over her features as she stared back at him.

Her face paled and her eyes went round. "I couldn't ruin…us."

The truth finally sat between them, thick and heavy. *The promise of more had always been at the edges of them.* "Better to not tempt us? You gave excuses. You wanted to pay your way. Live as much on your own as you could."

"Cods." She cleared her throat, turning to look out the windshield as they bumped along the backroads, trees and fields lining the way. "That was true. But, I didn't want to get hurt any more than I already was. Still don't."

"Your dad." It came out as a statement of fact. It stung, deep and to the core.

"I knew I liked you for a reason." But her joke fell flat.

"Yeah, I catch on like that. I'm also known as good time Cody, especially at The Giddy Up." He was also quick to realize a few other things and he didn't agree with them not one iota.

How could he convince Hannah they were better together than apart, though?

TWO HOURS IN the quiet cab with Cody unnerved her. She'd turned up the dial on the radio to fill the throbbing silence. Singing along in perfect harmony to the country songs put salve on her bruised feelings and strummed memories of road life between rodeos.

Now, Hannah beamed as she unhitched the latch and shoved open the squeaky metal trailer door. The restrained eighteen-hundred-pound bull shifted, kicking back.

"Whoa, now, Macho! Save that for the try out."

She shimmied her way along the inside wall to his head. "Good, bull." With gloved hands, she untied the rope that held him in place and clutched it in her hands. "Back out. Nice and easy now."

He flicked his head, barely raising his big brown eyes to her.

"Miss me? Is that why you're giving me the cold shoulder today?" Hannah used her forearm to nudge him backward.

His steps were agonizingly slow, but steady. Then midway in and out of the trailer, he halted. Flat-out stopped, digging in.

Men! "You're making me look bad here, Macho. You wouldn't want to do that, would you?" Bulls behaving badly were a norm in her world. If she could get him to contain that until the ring today...

"Need me to do anything, Hann?" Cody's calm, rock-steady voice stopped the ripple of bubbling panic in her belly.

"Smack him on the rump once and quick and then jump out of the way."

"Talk dirty to me, why don't you?" But she heard his smile.

Hannah chuckled. Doug Eastman and his two partners, watching from the top of the chute railing, joined in. She cringed. These were the guys who could hire Macho for the rodeo circuit.

"On three." Cody counted down and slapped the bull's hindquarters.

Macho kicked back once and then returned to his statue-like stance.

"Moody son-of-a-gun." He warned Hannah before trying again. This time the bull did move, forward.

His head lowered and Hannah jumped back and up, climbing the rail in the trailer. "Hey, now! Mama don't like that." She practically cooed, hoping he couldn't sense the pounding of her heart.

"Hann?"

"No worries." Her voice squeaked on a high note. She lowered her voice. "Now, you look here, Macho Man. I've got a reputation to uphold. You start getting that prima don attitude and I can't handle you, well, there goes my cash cow, er, bull, in this case. You are my moneymaker, got it? You scratch my back. I'll get cows to scratch your, uh, you-know-whats. Deal?"

The bull shoved forward, pinning her. Her grip tightened on the metal holds.

Hannah sucked in a breath.

Death by bull? Cripes, he outweighed her by a thousand seven hundred pounds! She'd be like a fly under his hoof—flat like a cow patty.

She'd spent the last five years of her life raising him and nine more like him, selling some to cull expenses for a bit. The heck she was going to go out like this.

"Back up." She grit her teeth. "Now! Move!"

Thankfully, he did. She jumped down, her boots hitting the trailer floor with a thud. Without stopping, she planted her hands on her hips and stepped forward as the bull walked backward.

"Go on! This is not new to you. Out the trailer. In the chute. To the ring."

Finally, she emerged from the back of the stuffy, smelly trailer as Cody grabbed the rope from her hand and got Macho to turn into the narrow metal chute and onward.

"Wow, Hannah! I've never seen a girl bully a bull into doing anything."

She stilled at the familiar voice coming from yards away. "Rodney?" *Why was he even here?* Glancing his way, she found him and his father, Senior, shoulder-to-shoulder at the rail. Dark hair and pale skin, neither looked like the fine weathered cowboys nearby.

"I'll buy him from you." The elder Ellis tipped back his cowboy hat. "But you come along with him as his trainer."

Shock surged through her veins. Cody stood frozen at her side now.

"Dad, really?" Rodney lost his coloring, going whiter than his normal look. "I can do it." He flicked a glance at her and Cody. "I don't need her."

"Hann?" Cody's whispered question stuck her as one of the nicest things anyone had done for her in this male-dominated world.

"Thanks for the offer, Mr. Ellis. But I'm keeping Macho. I can't get this close and sell him off, now can I?"

That was it. She'd poured so much of her grit and determination in to getting just the right bull. Hours upon hours of hard work followed, adding up to months and years. More bulls came along. But Macho was the best. She'd earned this.

"No convincing you, is there?" He stood straight, resignation in his sigh.

"'Fraid not."

"Thatta girl." Cody's soft words of praise warmed her.

"Gentlemen, ready to see what he's got?" She addressed the three men climbing down off the chute rail and watching Macho burst from the end and into the ring.

One of them whistled shrilly. Her bull rider friend and sometimes helper, Theo Graham, had showed up to help. His injury earlier this season sidelined him, but proved a godsend to her during Macho's auditions. "I'll make it a good ride, Hannah." He bumped fists with her.

"You better or I'm sunk."

"If you need me, I'll ride him for you." Cody's offer, stated low and only for her ears, surprised Hannah.

"You ride buckin' broncs, not bulls." Visions of him hitting the ground hard and being stomped on by Macho flashed through her head. "No. We're good. Thanks."

With Cody walking by her side and Theo and the guys setting up for the ride, Hannah prayed this was her day.

"He taking over the business?" Rodney fell in step on her left side. "Is that what the rumors are all about?"

Hannah cringed. He'd expected more from her. She dang well couldn't deliver, even if Cody wasn't in the picture.

"Rumors, Ellis?" There seemed an underlying challenge in Cody's question.

"The marriage kind." He chewed on a long piece of grass as usual. "Seems like we have some unfinished business, Hannah."

"Really? What could that be, Hann?"

She made it to the corral, climbing up on a rail to watch Butch and his brother Hank chase Macho into a pen. Satisfied, Theo grabbed his gear from the neat pile nearby and began slapping on his chaps.

Somehow Hannah felt like Macho did, shoved into a corner, pinned between two walls as Cody sat on one side of her and Rodney on the other, sitting far too close. His knee brushed hers.

"We had an understanding."

"There was a question, but no answer. Isn't that right, Hann?"

Why me?

"I've got a prenup ready and waiting."

Something cold and sharp dropped in her belly. "Why would you?"

"Protects both parties' interest."

Little ol' Hannah Prescott, after paying her rent and lease for her animals this month, had exactly eighty-five dollars in her checking account and slightly more in her savings. She rented a room. *One room!* Her banged up, used truck—paid for and all hers—wouldn't even get a decent blue book value if she'd totaled the thing tomorrow. Even the trailer she hauled had seen much better days. She might not have a whole heck of a lot, but she took pride in what she'd accomplished and how far she'd come.

All she had were her bulls. Market value would bring in a good sum, but nothing like Rodney Ellis and his family's fortunes.

Nope, he didn't care about protecting her at all.

"Heard you want to take over Hannah's bulls." Cody leaned forward to get a brief glance at a fidgeting Rodney on the other side of her.

"She needs a man to handle things."

Inside, she bristled. She clutched her hands on the rail, the wood digging into her palms and her fingernails practically stuck in it.

Cody threw back his head and laughed. "That's funny, Ellis, especially coming from you. A man?" He took pot shots at the pampered son of a wealthy man.

"And what do you have, McCall? Nothing. Not a thing. No buckin' broncs to ride. No rodeos to be a part of. No more prize money or buckles to win. Even less when you lose that ranch of your grandfather's. Maybe I'll have dad buy it once the bank forecloses on it."

Hannah reached over and clamped a hand on Cody's arm—his muscles bunching under her fingers—holding him back. *Or was she holding both of them back from punching Rodney's lights out.*

"The McCall ranch is staying right where it belongs. In McCall hands." Conviction rang in her voice.

That legacy would live on for generations to come. She didn't have that to honor and protect in her own family, but she'd be damned if she let Cody lose his family's life and breath.

"You sure about that, Hannah?" Ellis snickered.

"That's for damn sure." She turned to Cody, easing her hand from his forearm to lace her fingers with his.

A shot of electricity zinged up her arm. His eyes flared; he must have felt it, too.

"Because Cody McCall and I will save it together. That's what husbands and wives do. We protect the good, the right, the just. We stick by each other and we get through the good times and the bad times. We carry on. We are family. You can take that to the bank."

Yep, she just threw herself off that proverbial horse and was free falling off that cliff!

Chapter Fourteen

WITH HIS COWBOY hat in hand, Cody strolled through the lobby of the old grand hotel with its gleaming wood, sparkling chandeliers, lush carpeting, fancy furniture, and highly attentive staff.

This place wouldn't be his first choice to stay at overnight. But Gramps spoke so highly of it when he and Grams would come to town, Cody thought Hannah deserved to see something other than dusty truck cabs and seedy motels on the rodeo circuit.

"Where are you, Hann?" He glanced at the shiny-faced grandfather's clock in the corner. She never took this long to ever get ready.

Something had shifted this afternoon between them. She publicly declared their union. The fierce pride in her voice still beat in his chest.

His Hannah had made the commitment to be his wife.

Shock raced through him. He vowed to make her happy. Whatever it took.

Why hadn't he seen it long before now? Maybe losing so much shoved him into realizing he couldn't lose her, too. *I can't lose another piece of my heart.*

Cody nodded to the older couple passing him to go out for the evening. The man smiled widely and returned the nod, standing tall with his fine Stetson on his head and black, lariat tie and she—dressed in a fringed, white leather dress with colorful beads sewn on it—wore white matching cowgirl boots.

Would that be Hannah and him someday? He wanted forever. But she didn't count on anything permanent in her life after her folks died. It hurt too much, she'd said time and time again.

"Cods?" Her soft voice, coming from behind him, tugged at his heart.

Turning, he saw her standing there. Something curled, low and deep. "You look amazing, Hannah!"

Her simple black sleeveless blouse and short set were adorned with touches of gold—small hoop earrings, bracelet, and chain belt. A loose knot of hair piled on top of her head with little strands framing her face made her look damn sexy and he longed to pull the pins out to watch it tumble down. She wore just a touch of makeup and that rosy lip gloss he loved.

A humming sensation began in his body and increased as he swept a glance over her and lingered for a few moments on her bare legs before he took in her red cowgirl boots.

"Thanks, Cods." She bite her bottom lip. "You look mighty fine yourself, cowboy."

He'd packed his best shirt and jeans, polished his boots to a shine an hour ago, and prepared for their...

"Ready for our first real date?" He touched her elbow— the tingling turned up a notch—directing her to the door. They moved together, perfectly in sync as usual.

"Date? Sounds awkward." She put into words what they both felt. "So where are we going?

"Steak dinner after all your hard work today." On the sidewalk, he jutted his chin to the popular eatery across and down the street. "Been there before?"

"Can't say as I have. Kinda pricey. Just like the hotel. Are you sure about this?" She fell in step beside him, their boots hitting with a soft clatter.

"Gramps knows the owner and the guy owed him a favor. As for a meal, I think I can spring for that." He heard the smile in his own voice as he held her hand to cross the street, dodging the unusual flow of traffic for a weeknight. Another flicker of wonder rushed through him at the touch. "Afraid I can't keep you in the style you're accustomed to? Don't you worry, Miss Hannah Prescott, I'll have you back to your broken-down, beat-up piece of metal in no time flat. None the worse for wear."

Hannah chuckled. "And the cab full of snacks? Don't forget those."

He groaned. "How could I? Sweet addiction. Is there an AA meeting or something for that? We don't want to pass that down to our kids. You know, rotten teeth and all."

"Me? What about you, Cody McCall? You have a hole in that gut of yours." She skipped a few steps ahead, turned around, and then walked backward directly in front of him. Reaching out, she jabbed him in the stomach with a fisted hand. "Never full. Always on empty."

"I'm a growing guy. What can I say?"

They laughed together. He leaned down, even as they walked, cupped her cheeks in his hands and pressed a swift, hungry kiss on her lush lips. A fresh wave of desire swirled inside him. *God, he'd wanted to do that since the last one.*

"Cody? Is that you?" The strangled female voice stopped him cold.

Hannah halted in her tracks, too, so now she was pressed against him. Cody wrapped an arm around her to keep them both steady.

"It is you! And little Hannah!"

Frigid air swept over him at the woman glaring at them from three feet away. He hadn't seen her in nearly a year. She didn't even have the decency to send along her condolences or show up for Grams' funeral.

His lips tightened and his jaw ached. "Tabitha." He didn't recognize the two cowboys with her. It didn't matter. She'd always had some guy hanging on to her every word. At one time, even him.

HANNAH STOOD FROZEN to the spot. The very beautiful, dark-haired Tabitha didn't blink. Her blue eyes nearly bugged out of her head. That made Hannah laugh. She received another rather pointy glare.

"I knew it! You two had something going on even back then."

Reluctantly, Hannah stepped back from Cody—tension in every line of his tall, gorgeous body. Alarm bells blared in her head. She became aware they were drawing attention from passersby. "If you need to talk with her, Cods…"

Her throat closed up; she couldn't finish her words or stop her wayward thoughts. They'd been a couple. *Did he wish they still were? If they had a chance, would he take it?* After all, Cody hadn't been the one to end it.

Dread gathered low in her stomach. A memory of her mother in a similar position with the other woman—or rather, women, as in the plural form—flashed in her mind. *History repeating itself!*

"If you'll excuse us." Cody directed Hannah away and continued on their path.

"Wait!" Tabitha's voice hitched. She caught up with them. Her hand landed on Cody's arm. "We should." Her gaze cut to Hannah.

"All that needed saying was said. But if you need to speak, Hannah's not going anywhere." He reached down and laced his fingers with Hannah's. He squeezed hers.

Was it for her reassurance or his?

"We had something, Cody." Now she spent more time glancing between Hannah and Cody, obviously gauging their reactions. "*You* wanted *me*."

"I was wrong." His words, softly spoken, dropped like bullets between them.

Her mouth opened and closed. "But…" She frowned.

Not a good look! The crinkles between her brows and the storm gathering in her eyes marred her gorgeous rodeo queen features.

"It's always been Hannah for me."

She smirked. "And you conveniently forgot while you were with me."

"Something like that." He sighed. "Give my best to your folks." Cody nodded to her, to the two cowboys who stood back, and then wrapped his arm around Hannah's shoulder as he guided her away from the scowling woman.

It hadn't ended this nicely with her mother. Her haunting cries when her father's girlfriend at the time laughed in her face still echoed in Hannah's ears. "Sure about this?" Hannah asked under her breath.

"Hell, yeah." His strained voice sat between them, thick and pulsing.

Eerie silence followed them to the wood and glass door of the restaurant. Hannah snuck a peek back and saw Tabitha with her hands on her hips shooting daggers at them. *Cripes!*

The muted sounds of the steakhouse filled in the void

between Cody and her. Murmured conversations, softly clinking glasses, and silverware played like a musical instrument.

In a few moments, they were shown to their table. Hannah eyed the place—elegant with a touch of hunting lodge tossed in. "Nice, especially without the hanging animal heads and their beady eyes staring down at us."

Cody laughed, gruff and quick. "That mountain place, right? Creepy."

A slim vein of relief shot through her. She flipped open the leather menu. "What's good?"

"Steak." His deadpan response made her giggle.

"Funny, Cods." She glanced at him from under her lashes and the knot in her belly slipped a tad at the smile playing around his lips. *Oh, those firm, skillful lips she wanted to taste again.*

"Know what you want yet?"

"Steak." She chuckled and he joined in.

He folded up his menu, got up, and then came to her side of the table, nudging her to slid over along the booth seat.

"What?" But she did, allowing him in.

"Too far away, Hann." He looped an arm along the back of the booth. Cody trailed his fingers on her shoulder before settling there. "Did I ever tell you that you make me laugh?"

"I'm a barrel of fun, didn't you know that?" She suppressed the shiver from his touch; however, the heat remained. Cupping a hand to the side of her mouth, she said, "Psst! Don't tell anyone, but I do a mean chicken dance."

They burst out laughing.

Visions of pairing up for their friends' weddings rushed back to her. If they weren't in the wedding party, they'd been invited. To stop their well-intentioned buddies from playing wedding guest matchmakers, Cody and she made a pact they'd go to the shindigs together, never solo. A good time was had by all, including drinking games, silly dances— on the floor and on top of the tables—and snitching lots of wedding cake leftovers.

"The best times yet the worst bridesmaid's dresses and ruffled shirts."

She groaned. "Don't remind me. Well, the awful pictures are etched in our history."

"Tell me about it. I bribed and stole a few of the really incriminating ones of us."

"Cods, you'd do that for me? Ah…what a sweetheart of a guy you are." It seemed safer this way, the friendship thing.

"Yeah, Hann, I'd do anything for you." He leaned in, brushing his lips against hers.

The room spun. She clutched at the front of his shirt. "You don't play fair, Cods."

"All's fair in love…" He stole another kiss, this one a second longer, but just as hot.

She trembled. His face—rugged and so endearing to

her—was mere inches away now. "Friends, first." It came out half question, half plea. "We can never let anything damage that."

"That's who we are. That's what we stand on to build a life together."

"Promise?" Doubts niggled at the back of her mind and the edges of her heart.

HER QUESTION NEEDED answering. He'd put it off long enough for the waiter to bring their meals, refill their drinks, and then move on to the next table of new arrivals.

Cody tried to put it short and simple as he cut into his thick, juicy porterhouse. "Out of everyone I know, you've never let me down." His parents had by dying. Grams had by getting sick and dying. His Gramps mortgaged the very ranch Cody had called home all his life. His brothers didn't seem as concerned at the moment to do something about any of it, too.

She cringed and then dug in to her meal. "Even with Tabitha?"

Like most women, she wanted to know. "Especially with her." He took a moment to chew on his thoughts as well as his delicious steak. The memory of that time filled him with dread. "You backed off." Losing her felt like someone had ripped his heart right out of his chest. *Hollow. Empty.*

"I did it for you. Even though I'm not the girl's biggest fan, I am yours. I want you happy."

"And that's the crux of everything." He used his burgundy cloth napkin to wipe the corner of his mouth.

"Happy?"

"That and you."

"Me?" She dropped her fork. It hit the plate with a clatter. The family of three nearby turned. Hannah shot them a smile of apology and focused on him again. "Not my plan."

"It was hers. To get you out of my life." He took a long sip of his beer, licked his lips, and then set it back down. "Conditions. You were top of the list. Either you were gone or we were done."

Her face paled. "I suspected it, but didn't think she'd said it to your face."

"Plain and clear."

"What else?"

"Isn't that enough?"

Hannah ignored her cola and reached over and took a sip of his beer. "That is way better. Okay, tell me."

"It wasn't so much requests, but demands. Move off the ranch. More of the rodeo life. The king and queen of the circuit, I think she emphasized. No kids for five years."

"Wow, she doesn't ask for much, does she?" Hannah glanced at him with her big, brown eyes.

A tiny shiver tickled his spine. He nearly moaned. "Hann." Her name caught in the back of his throat. "I didn't care about the rest, not after she harped on you."

She frowned. "You love the ranch…"

"I'd never have given it up or walked away. What I'm saying is, once she made it known you could no longer be a part of my life, I made my decision. The rest of the list was just background noise."

Her brows went up and her eyes rounded.

"That's right. I refused to comply. She pouted. She stomped her feet. Both. Yeah, not attractive at all." He grimaced. "I hit the road."

"But…she…you…I thought—"

"Spit it out, honey." He grinned at her unusual lack of a comeback.

"Why didn't you tell me this last year?"

"She put the story out there." He shrugged. "I was wrapped up with Grams and then Gramps and then the ranch. By the time I found out, I didn't care. Who was I to make her look like a fool? I figured the people who knew me best would know I wasn't pining for her."

"But you're different."

"I barely escaped, Hann. What was I thinking?" Now, he wondered about it even more. With Hannah right in front of him, how could he have even looked at another woman? "She's shallow and needy. Two things I don't want in a wife."

"Are, I mean, *were* you shopping for one?" That question, sharp and quick, made him chuckle.

"Ah, sarcasm, how I've missed you."

She jabbed him in the ribs with an elbow.

Cody rubbed his side. "Dang, girl, that pointy thing is dangerous."

Her glance flickered over him. "I wouldn't be talking about pointy things, if I were you."

They chuckled in unison. But something low and deep inside him curled tighter at the pink sweeping over her cheeks. Warmth turned to heat in a split second.

"You feel that?" Her whisper-soft words were like a feather trailing over his skin.

Leaning close, he moaned. "Dang, girl, right here? For shame."

Hannah laughed, soft and low.

Pulling away slightly, he looked into her sparkling eyes. "This makes me happy. *You* make me happy."

"Same here. You do that for me, too."

"So let's get hitched. Soon."

She sucked in a sharp, shaky breath.

"It's me, Hann. Trust *me*. Trust in *us*."

Could she put aside all her misgivings?

Chapter Fifteen

HANNAH DRAGGED CODY down the sidewalk a few blocks, and then down a side street and toward the bar where lively country music rang out, blaring louder each time someone opened the door. "Come on, life of the party! Let's go dance."

"Celebrate?"

Her answer stuck, so she nodded and tugged him along the wooden planks. His boot steps matched hers now.

Fear nearly strangled her. She didn't want to lose him— now or later.

For most of her life, she'd watched her mom cater to her dad's whims. He was loving and a good dad—patient, kind, and spending time with her. *Not so much a husband.* Her folks bought, sold out, or lost every business they'd started. But that wasn't the half of it. Nope, her mom turned a blind eye to her dad's many affairs as he drifted along the rodeo circuit. *Even after bumping into him and his girlfriends!* His charming ways and big smile won over many, while some just flat out threw themselves at him.

She'd seen it time and time again with her own eyes. It

wasn't like he hid it from anyone.

No, her daddy was not a one-woman man.

Many a time, she'd be the one to console her mom as she cried on Hannah's shoulder. It tore a hole in Hannah's heart, bigger and wider each time.

But her mother didn't know any other kind of life or didn't want to bother to dig deep and piece together her shattered dignity.

Years ago, Hannah promised herself she'd never end up like that, not beholden to a man. Ever.

Now, look at her! Giddiness at being near Cody McCall bubbled up inside her. Her pulse galloped in her neck. Her breath hitched like she'd been dancing all night long.

I'm scared, Cods!

At the door of the Swig and Swirl bar—where the motto was, swig a beer and swirl your girl—Cody stopped her. Facing her, he looked into her eyes.

She sucked in a sharp breath at the love and devotion shining in his eyes.

"Be my wife, Hann."

An image of his Gramps and Grams flashed through her mind. "Like Left and Winnie McCall? What they had?"

His brow knitted over his beautiful eyes. "I wouldn't have it any other way."

Hannah let out the pent-up air in her lungs. It came out in a whoosh. "You, Cody McCall, have yourself a deal." She grinned even as her chin wobbled.

Please, don't let this be the worst mistake of our lives. Please, let this work. What would I do without Cody?

"One week, Hann. That's all we're giving them to plan our wedding. Then I get you for my bride." He dropped a tender kiss on her forehead and then opened the door for her.

Music, light, and loud voices blasted her, along with her many doubts.

Hannah shoved everything aside, crossed the threshold while tugging Cody along, and then hit the floor dancing.

He fell in step easily to the rowdy tune. His holler cut through the air and others joined his. Some of the guys and girls they knew called out their names.

"Yo, Cody!"

"Hannah, save one for me!"

On the outskirts of the dance floor, she spotted Tabitha twirl around and gaze at them, her beautiful, expressive features revealing the stab of envy. She immediately reached out for the nearest cowboy and hooked her elbow through his, smiling sweetly.

In that moment, Hannah thanked the heavens that Cody had seen the truth about Tabitha before it was too late.

Silently, she wished the girl all the best in finding whatever, or whoever, she was searching for to make her happy.

Just like that Hannah blocked out everyone else and focused on her soon-to-be groom. HIs grin only made the small dimple in his chin more attractive. And the light in his eyes brought her some hope. Maybe they could pull this one off...

HER HEAD BUZZED. She couldn't be certain, but the town swayed to the left and then to the right as they walked back to the hotel. *Motion sickness?* "Those last couple hundred dances with the strobe lights flashing—when did they put up that disco ball? Not such a good idea." Her feet burned in protest.

Cody halted and then had her climb on. "Piggyback ride."

"Good ol' Cods to the rescue again."

He hiked her up higher.

"Whoa! My head spun and my belly flip-flopped." She wrapped an arm around his throat.

"Choking me."

"Oops!" She loosened her grip. "Sorry." Closing her eyes, she laid her head on his shoulder, pressing her face against his neck. His shiver made her smile. *At least we have that!* She snuggled closer.

His heavy footsteps echoed in her pounding temples. His warmth seeped in to her chilly, bare legs. Awareness of where his large hands were—on her bare thighs and then one of them back to her butt to readjust her as she slid down with each step.

"Is this foreplay, Cody?" She giggled. "'Cause that feels good."

His moan rumbled against her palm as she clutched him, her fingers dug in to the front of his shirt.

"Speechless? Not like you at all."

"Ah, hate to tell you this, Hann, but we have onlookers."

"Peepers?" She shifted her head on his shoulder and blinked her eyes open. Bright light nearly blinded her. They were walking through the hotel lobby now, getting some mighty fine stares from at least a dozen people—staff and travelers alike. Hannah waved and then quickly grabbed Cody again as she slipped. "Hey, folks! Nice night, isn't it?"

Some older cowboy tipped his hat—at Cody or her, she couldn't be certain. A few of the hotel staff members ducked as they grinned from ear-to-ear. The woman half of a nearby couple gasped and turned her back.

"Fans?" She snorted and then erupted in giggles.

"She wishes she could." He strode to the elevator door, pressed the button, and then waited for the doors to part as they dinged open.

Hannah looked up in time to see the college-aged, elevator attendee's jaw drop and eyes pop out of his head. He stuttered. "Sir...ma'am." But he held the door and gawked as Cody carried her in.

"Fifth floor."

Soon the soft thud of the doors shutting broke the silence. The compartment closed in on them—tight and suffocating—as it moved silently upward.

"I hate that part." She couldn't breathe and that spinning thing was happening again.

"Don't get sick on me, Hann."

She gulped back a tide of rising nausea. "Yuck! Vrrp!"

"So attractive when she's in the throes of motion sickness, isn't she?" Cody chuckled and the attendee looked away as he smiled.

"Tastes better going down then it does coming back up."

"Yep, that's my bride." But his voice held a well of pride in it.

Hannah laughed all the way to her door.

Gingerly, he eased her down and on her feet. Her legs wobbled.

Was it from the dizziness or because of him?

Cody propped her against the wall as he felt for key cards in his pocket, found hers, inserted it in the slot, jammed down on the door handle, and then kicked it open for her. "In you go. Remember, cool compresses to your forehead and back of your neck does the trick." He gently wrapped his warm fingers around her cold upper arms—leaving a very nice thrill behind—directed her into the room, nudged her away and back, and then tossed her a key card. He waved as the door swung closed. "Nightie night."

"Huh?" But the big wooden thing-a-ma-gig separated them now. "Cods?"

"I don't do sick first times. Understand?"

Clutching the card—the sharp edges digging into her flesh—Hannah leaned her forehead against the cool cherry wood. "Yeah. Got it."

"Good." His voice faded away.

"I'm saving myself for our wedding night!"

"Oh, dear!" A female voice answered.

Her head shot up. Her feet shifted. She shoved down hard on the handle and jerked open the door to come face-to-face with an older woman dressed in a fringed white cowgirl outfit leaning on her cowboy's arm, who wore matching attire. The woman's softly wrinkled face still held shock. "You heard." Hannah cringed.

"In my day, we didn't have to announce it, dear."

"Of course not." A jabbing sensation rippled through her middle. Hannah sucked in a fresh breath, and then another, sweeping away the nausea. She slinked back, inching the door closed again. "Goodnight." Peeking out, she watched as the couple slowly disappeared down the hall and around the corner.

Peering first to the left and then to the right, she found no one else in the hall. She scurried out. Her door shut with a definite click. Thankfully, her head was clearing and the sound didn't ricochet through her. Cody's room loomed near. Before she lost her nerve, she knocked once.

There was no answer.

With a shaky breath, she rapped her knuckles louder. The noise echoed in the hall. Hannah searched around, making certain it remained empty.

She focused again and frowned. Pressing her ear against his door, she listened.

Not a sound!

"Maybe it's for the best." She backed away and walked briskly to her room. Taking her key card, she stuck it in the slot. The light blinked red. "Seriously? You're a little chip in a plastic card." Trying again, she yanked it out and jammed it back in over and over with the same result. "Oh, for the love of—"

Hannah stilled. She glanced down at the card, peeked over her shoulder to Cody's room, looked back, and then shook her head. "No. You couldn't have."

She tried again. She failed again.

That sinking sensation dropped in her belly. "Could he have?" There was only one way to find out for certain.

"Go ahead. Ruin my night." She grit her teeth as she marched back to Cody's room. Out of politeness, she knocked again. Not a thing stirred. However, now she heard water running. Visions of him wet and naked under the warm spray of the shower teased every place on her, making her tingle.

Muttering under her breath, Hannah shoved the key card in his lock. The green light taunted her.

"No, no, no!"

It vanished.

She repeated inserting the card. *Green flashy light, of*

course!

With hesitant steps, she entered. The door shut behind her, like a death knell. The sound of rushing water blasted her ears. "Cods? It's me. Funny thing…" Her words died in the back of her throat at the sight before her.

The large jacuzzi tub in the room—with jets on high and the rising water frothy and swirling—enveloped Cody McCall. From her vantage point, she noted his bare chest and his lean six pack abs.

Too bad the water was so high.

He lounged back, with his head on a white towel and his eyes closed. A tiny smile played around his mouth, like he dreamed about something sweet and delicious.

Hannah licked her dry lips as she moved closer.

Over the years, there had been plenty of times she'd seen him shirtless. However, this was different. *Intimate.*

"You just going to stand there and stare?"

She gasped. "Playing possum, Cods?"

He opened one eye, his smile growing. "I took yours by mistake and had my extra." He nodded to the tossed key cards on the dresser. "You were supposed to stay in your room."

"Like a good little girl."

"You?" He chuckled, shifting and turning off the faucets. Only the hum of the jacuzzi remained. "No, Hann, so you'd sleep."

"I'm feeling better." Somewhere between him dropping

her off at her room and now, she'd shaken the dizzy effect. She kicked off a boot and then tugged the other one off, they hit the lush carpet with a dull thud. Her hands trembled as she went for the gold chain belt at her waist.

"Are you doing what I think you're doing?"

His voice, low and husky, strummed a chord deep inside her. "Hell, yes, Mr. McCall." Her courage increased at his loud swallow.

"I've got Gramps to answer to."

The metal clinked as it fell to the floor. "And is that *my* problem?" She grinned, unbuttoning her black, sleeveless blouse to reveal her lace and satin black bra.

"What about Miss Peaches and Miss Clementine? We'll have to face them." His glance dropped briefly and then back up to capture her stare.

"Damn," she muttered, halting. "Forgot." Shrugging, she decided it was worth the grief.

She slid the blouse off one shoulder and then the other. The sound of her unsnapping her hook seemed deafening. She clutched the loose garment to her and shimmied out of her shorts.

"Hann." The warning in his voice bounced all around them.

It fueled her on. "We can play, can't we?" She dropped her hand and her bra fluttered to her feet.

He cursed. "You are dangerous." But his heated gaze lingered.

Warmth and desire swirled, spurring her on. She dropped her hands to the band around her hips.

"Not your panties, Hannah. I can barely keep it together now."

She giggled, liking the way his eyes lit up. "Scared?"

"Hell, yeah." His gulp reached her. "You got protection? 'Cause I don't."

"You didn't bring any?" That brought on two totally different reactions—disappointment and delight.

"I didn't plan on seducing you here."

"Oh, Cody! That's just the sweetest thing." She did as he asked and left her panties on.

Going to him, Hannah climbed in the delicious, steaming water of the jacuzzi and straddled his lower thighs. *Hot, wet skin and strong muscles.* His hands gripped the sides of the tub.

"What? That turns you on even more?" The corner of his mouth twitched upward.

"Call me crazy, Cody McCall, but when a guy doesn't have any intention of getting me drunk and having his way with me, it's a huge turn-on."

"Go figure!"

Tilting up his chin with her forefinger, she gazed into his warm, shining green eyes. She bit her bottom lip. "Thanks."

Her heart melted. He was a rare breed of men. *Proud. Honorable. Hers.*

"No one has ever treated me as good as you." That truth

snuck into her core and spread, exploding in wonder. Tears stung her eyes. Leaning toward him, her hair swinging forward, Hannah gently brushed his lips with hers.

"Sweet torture."

"Good thing we didn't bring anything or else..." She teased his mouth, staying longer this time.

Tension rippled through him. "Play today, Hann. But you just wait for our wedding night."

Tiny thrills raced up and down her spine. "Promise, Cods?"

"You can bank on it. I never break a promise."

Another blast of realization stormed through her, tugging her in the deepest places and shedding hope. "Yeah, I knew that."

Cody never let her down. *He wouldn't start now, would he?*

Chapter Sixteen

A BLAST OF heat swept over Hannah's cheeks as she stood with Cody at the hotel checkout counter. Flashes of Cody carrying her on his back across this very lobby snapped through her mind, like lightning. *What exactly had she done last night?*

"Did you enjoy your stay with us, Miss Prescott? Mr. McCall?" The clerk—Ned, by his name tag—casually glanced from her and then to Cody.

The warmth rose, turning to a slow burn. *Did she!* "Love-ly, old chap." She relied on her wit and exaggerated English accent to divert from her twinge of embarrassment.

His mouth twitched.

Cody chuckled.

That husky sound rushed through her and left blazing trails behind. She ached in all the right places.

Memories of being in that jacuzzi with him, teasing, playing, and kissing him deep and long slammed into her.

He must have felt her quiver; he looped an arm around her waist, brushing his thumb along her side, and then pressed a gentle kiss on her head.

Her Cody had finally put a halt to it—literally and figuratively pulling the plug. In true gentlemanly style, he'd rubbed her dry with a big, white fluffy towel, gotten her one of his shirts to wear, and tucked her into his bed. And Cody—in nothing but his unbuttoned jeans—had hunkered down in the armchair with his feet resting on the end of the bed. He guarded her the entire night.

It was the first time since her parents' accident she could recall she didn't have a bad dream.

"Ready?" He turned to her, tucking the paperwork in his top pocket.

"Road trip and snacks? Do you even have to ask?"

His eyes captured hers. She swallowed hard at the hot, intense stare. Promises lingered, sweet and enticing. Hannah gasped.

He winked and his grin stretched wider. "Who knew, Hann? If we just let our guards down ages ago…"

Tiny thrills went down her spine. "Ah, hate to tell you this, but talking like that and looking at me like that, well, it just makes it a whole lot worse."

Cody picked up their overnight bags and nodded to the entrance. "So, I guess that leaves out necking in the truck at a couple of pit stops on the way home."

"Torture?"

They groaned in unison as they crossed the threshold to exit.

"Yoo hoo!" Miss Peaches stormed them, followed by

Sandy and Julie.

Hannah froze in her tracks. She spotted the burgundy jalopy at the curb. "I'm seeing things."

"What the hell?" Cody dropped the bags at his feet. They landed with a thunk.

Miss Peaches—decked out in a vibrant pink dress with matching accessories—flung herself at Hannah. She squeezed her in a suffocating embrace.

"Ah, bones. Fragile."

Her arms, like bands of steel, crushed her. "Oh dear, don't tell Clem, but the girls and I broke out and want to take you dress shopping."

Finally, Hannah eased away from the clinging, uncomfortable hug. "How did you know where we were?"

"Left called to let us know at curfew time last night. Thank goodness, I picked up and not Sister. I went straight to work, calling your friends."

Sheepishly, Sandy and Julie inched up their hands and waved their fingers while grimacing. "Surprise! Wedding dress. Remember?"

Hannah's heart sank. Miss Peaches' idea of a dress and hers were centuries apart. Her friends were more like fancy and frilly.

"I'll leave you beauties to all those lady things." Cody swept up the bags, dropped a swift kiss on her lips, and then walked backward along the sidewalk. "Don't worry, Hann. You'll be fine. I'll get the truck and go load up Macho in the trailer."

"Do not leave town without me, Cody McCall!" Her fierce warning rang out.

"Ah, the snack addition again." He shook his head.

"I mean it. Give me two hours then you come find me."

"Two? That's all?" Miss Peaches voice sank.

Holding up her hand, Hannah flicked up her index finger. "One." Then she held up her second finger alongside the first. "Two."

"Got it." Cody grinned. "I guess that gives me time to find some chocolate, too."

"Don't you know it!" The block of panic shifted in her chest. "Super-size the candy bars, too!"

She was going to need something extra sweet and lasting to get over the sawdust taste in her mouth after the grueling shopping excursion.

This was getting way too real for her!

HANNAH DIDN'T HAVE the heart to rain on Miss Peaches' parade. The woman glowed! *Even after their third stop.*

"You'd think she was the one getting hitched," she muttered to Sandy on the other side of the rack of gorgeous gowns.

"Right?" She held up a big, puffy-sleeved one. "Like it?"

"Not in the least." She had seen a simple one as she

walked in. *White. Lace. Off the shoulder. Mid-length. Perfect for wearing cowgirl boots with.*

"Wow, did you see these prices, Hann?"

She flipped over the slim card. "Ouch! Sticker shock." Her bank account wouldn't even cover the sales tax.

"Don't you worry about that, dear." Miss Peaches hugged her from behind.

"Ah, less of touchy-feely please." Of the two sisters, this one was the more demonstrative. Thankfully, she'd kept it to a minimum over the years.

The older woman giggled, but eased away. "You're so silly, Hannie."

"And you are giddy."

"That I am. You're like a niece to me, dear." She sniffled.

A thick lump stuck in Hannah's throat. "Thanks."

Sandy pointed a thumb over her shoulder. "I think that's Julie calling for me. She may need help trying on those half dozen dresses she's eyeing for her own future wedding." Backing away, she cringed as Miss Peaches soft cries began.

Traitor!

Hannah sighed and then turned fully to the sweet lady. "There, there, Miss Peaches." She guided her to a nearby chair and then sank down in the one beside it, gently and awkwardly patting the older woman on her back.

"It's just...I love weddings." But her tears fell faster and harder. "Oh, pooh! I have a confession to make."

"You?" She plucked out a few tissues from the box on the

table at her elbow and handed them over.

"Once, many years ago, I was to be a bride."

Jerking her head back, Hannah asked, "Like in marriage?"

"Yes." It wobbled out along with a puff of a chuckle. "He was so handsome. My Gerald."

Why hadn't she ever heard of this before? "Why didn't you go through with it?"

Her heavy sigh whooshed out. "Choices. I felt sorry for Clem. She had no one. Gerald was attending medical school. He and I were going to build a life in Houston. He's a highly sought after surgeon now," she whispered the last, but her voice shook with pride.

So, she'd kept up with his career. "Married?"

"Widowed young. Two children. Four grandchildren." Another sigh escaped. "He came back. He asked me again. I could have loved him and his children even after he lost his wife."

"But you said no. Because of Miss Clementine." She blurted out the cold, hard truth.

"I could have lived my dreams." Reaching over, she grabbed Hannah's hands in hers. "Some dreams you don't even know you have until they're gone. Age does that to you. Makes you realize what you truly wanted and didn't go after. Don't let that happen to you, my dear Hannah."

Numb, she gazed at the sweet woman who seemed to have grown older right before her. Pretty blue eyes that once shone with hope appeared dull and listless now.

Is that what happens when love dies inside you? Is that the way I'll look in years to come if I don't risk it all now?

WORKING ALWAYS SOOTHED Cody's mind. It didn't today or yesterday or the day before that. In fact, ever since that night with Hannah last week at the hotel all he could think of was her.

Sexy as hell!

She'd always been. He just didn't openly acknowledge that fact to himself or anyone else. It was safer that way.

The cattle nearby mowed.

"Yeah, yeah. I hear ya." He used the pitchfork to break up a fresh bale of hay for the dozen or so cows pressing close. "Don't ruin your dinner now with all this snacking."

The gruff laughter behind him jerked Cody's attention away from the feeding.

He eyed his grandfather swaggering up to the fence with Sweet Potato trotting beside him. Gramps' trusty utility vehicle sat quiet yards away. "Gramps. How long you been there?"

"Long enough to know you got something chewing at you."

"You read minds, too?"

He took off his Stetson, scratched his head, and then

plopped it back on. "Nope. Wish I did. I'd be richer than those oil barons. They're dead and still making money hand over fist." His weary sigh whistled through the air.

"Another notice?" His middle clutched.

He'd paid the latest installment, or so he'd thought, but the past due amount was another thing. Plus, Cody had finally gotten his brothers' attention. Caleb covered the utilities and more with his paycheck this week. And Conner worked twice as hard as anyone on the ranch, making up for not being able to hire more hands.

As soon as things settled down some, they planned on getting Gramps to fess up to the entire debt to discuss payments and options.

Cody swiped a hand over his forehead as he walked to his grandfather. "You're not smiling."

"And you're not singing or dancing like you usually do."

"You going to tell me or do I need to guess again?" They'd played this little game a few months ago until Gramps finally spilled it.

"The bank."

That was it. His jaw tensed and the muscle along it jumped. "How much?" The late fees and interest were piling up, the numbers boggling.

"Low clouds. Hope they pass by before your and Hannah's big day this weekend."

With a knot in his gut, he went along with his grandfather. "Thanks, Gramps, for letting us have the ceremony here on the ranch." He didn't want it any other way. Hannah didn't either. This was home. *How long would they have it for though?*

"Nice of Juan and Rosa to move into the big house and let you two newlyweds have the tiny one."

"*Johnny* and *Rose* insisted. They want to keep an eye on you." He delivered it with a smile, but he knew the devoted couple worried endlessly about Gramps' well-being, too.

"Well, it's a lot better than Hannah and you having to move in with this old coot, don't you think? You young'uns need your own place."

"I don't know. God knows why, but Hannah has a sweet spot for you, old coot or no coot."

That got a good chuckle out of his grandfather. "I always liked that girl."

"Me, too." *More than like.*

He sobered. "Shame what happened. Your Grams and I wanted to take her in. Hannie refused. I guess she hurt a whole lot more than she let most of us see. But you knew that. The crushing pain you don't let anyone witness. Best to stop feeling, stop loving the ones who can leave and rip your heart out the next time. You reading between the lines, son?"

"You push the ones you love away." Cody gazed out over the land and the grazing cattle. The stampede had robbed him of his parents. He grit his teeth.

"So you don't get hurt again." Gramps finished. "You got each other and—" He choked up and then cleared his throat, patting Cody on his arm. "You remember what you have doesn't come along but once in a blue moon. You and Hannah remind me of Grams and me. Don't you two screw that up, you hear?"

Cody laughed. "And here I thought you were getting all mushy on me, Gramps."

"Me? Never! Gotta keep up the act, right?" He shoved away from the corral fence. "Come on, Sweet Potato, let's go check on the wedding prep."

He watched his proud grandfather gaze around the property, taking in the sweeping fields, the high ridge in the distance, the barn and outbuildings, Grams' gardens, and then settle on the big house. *His and Grams.*

Gramps' heavy sigh floated to him even from here.

A ripple of fresh panic went through him.

How could he stop the bank from taking the ranch? Looking at Gramps' haggard face as he climbed back into the vehicle, Cody witnessed the air of defeat.

An invisible hand clutched Cody's heart.

He couldn't allow their home to slip away. There had to be a way to save it. *And save Gramps.*

"SERIOUSLY? WHAT ARE you doing here?" Hannah stuck her head out her bedroom window. "Is this like reliving memories? One for the road?" She glanced over her shoulder, hearing Miss Peaches and Miss Clementine chattering in the parlor with Mr. Samuels.

In the darkness, she could only make out Cody's blond hair and tall frame.

"Cods? You backing out?" Her heart jumped to her throat. The night before a wedding usually the bride or groom got cold feet.

"Hann, you think I'd do that to you?"

She blew out a pent-up breath. Hannah dropped to her knees and rested her arms on the sill. "No, no. What's up?"

"I can't stop thinking about you."

Warmth ricocheted from her chest to her cheeks and back again. "Like in the jacuzzi thinking?"

His low chuckle caused another bolt of heat to rush through her veins. "Hannah Prescott, tsk tsk."

Now her face burned. "What? I can't ask?"

"Yes, I want you. More than I ever realized."

"Good to know. Same here." The words were thick with need.

Cody stepped closer, gazing up at her. "Hann. You're my best friend. I don't want that to change. We should get better together."

Thoughts whirled in her mind. Memories flared. Her mother's cries rushed back. "Can we?"

"You and me, Hannah."

His vow sounded like music to her ears.

"I'm pledging my heart to you tomorrow. All of it. No

fences. I just want the same from you."

"All I can do is try."

"Try harder, Hann. Fight for it and us!"

His fierce words echoed through the still, dark night.

"I know you. I know you're scared and you have doubts. I need you on my side on this. I've got the ranch to save. Yeah, the bills are rolling in and there's no money to pay all of them. It will be months before we go through the season and sell a bunch of the cattle at market."

Something inside her began to burn. The McCalls couldn't possibly lose what was theirs. *Not the ranch. Not their home.* It wasn't fair or right. Now, she could focus. "You got me. We'll do this."

Why didn't that ease the tension?

"Cods?"

"All in, Hann. I mean it. You're great when something needs to get done—ranching, raising bulls—the physical hard work. But…"

He stepped closer, so now the arch of light from her room bathed him. His eyes, lit from within, caused her stomach to drop and then bounce up to her ribs. It hurt to draw in a breath.

"Nothing less than your whole heart, Hannah. I'm here to tell you not to show up tomorrow if you can't give me that."

Chapter Seventeen

CODY RODE OUT on his horse as dawn broke. Streaks of red and orange painted the sky. The soft clops of the hooves hitting the ground and the easy familiar sway were soothing to his jangled nerves.

He had no idea if Hannah would follow through today or not.

That troubled him because he couldn't figure out if he'd gotten to her last night. Her silence had beat down on him and he'd left her there.

The gentle breeze brought the scent of fresh cut grass. Yellows, mixed with oranges, yawned from the horizon. His smile came with ease and without thought.

Looking at the ridge, he spotted the newly built, temporary altar decked with flowers and the rows and rows of chairs. His insides jumped in a mixture of anticipation and worry.

In a matter of hours, he'd discover if all the hard work his family and friends had done putting the pieces together had been worth it. Aunt Sissy, Uncle Jeb, and his cousins worked hardest of all.

Maybe he pushed Hannah too much. The boundaries Hann put up over the years seemed to pile higher and higher. Her life revolved around her stock contracting business. Buying, training, and breeding the best bulls in this part of the country proved successful and rewarding.

Dating cowboys disappointed her more and more. They'd let her down. Every last one wanted to change her to fit their wants and needs.

Could he show her he wasn't like them?

The sound of horse's galloping up behind him jerked Cody around in his saddle. He chuckled at the sight of his brothers coming toward him.

As they drew closer, they eased their rides into a slow trot to match his. "The McCall brothers." Caleb's short explanation said it all.

They'd banded together from birth—the code of honor and family first—strong to their cores.

Cody never felt so proud as he did at this moment riding between his oldest brother, Caleb, to the right of him and his youngest brother, Conner, to the left of him.

They gazed out over the sweeping hills, dipping valleys, and magnificent oak trees. The love of the lush land their family had bought, worked hard to cultivate, sacrificed everything to succeed, and that their parents had given their lives for beat strong and fierce in their blood.

He nudged his horse to a halt, taking it all in. Cody pictured his children and their children in years to come gazing out over their land just as his brothers and he were now. "This is our legacy to keep and to pass down."

"Damn straight it is," Connor and Caleb said in unison.

"Whatever it takes."

A renewed sense of urgency grabbed hold of Cody. He longed for this, for Hannah and his kids. His heart lurched in his chest at the image of Hannah holding their baby.

He could give her a family. They could make this their home.

But will she let me in to love her like she needs to be loved?

THE SUN, WARMING his shoulders, climbed a little higher in the sky as Cody led his brothers back to the ranch.

"I figured Caleb would be the first to bite the bullet." Connor grinned.

"Watch out. You may be next if Aunt Sissy has anything to say about it." Caleb pointed to the line of trucks kicking up dust in the distance as they came down the ranch road. "Yep, that's her now with her posse in tow."

"She's got three of her own to matchmake for, so why me?"

Cody chuckled. "Just lucky, I guess."

"Or bad luck of the draw."

"Well, brother, you can always take the easy way out and hightail it out of Dodge. We need someone at the base camp for a few weeks. With me getting hitched…" He trailed off, wondering if he might just need some time to himself if his bride ditched him.

"I'll take it. Anything to shift her focus off me and put it back on the cousins."

He made out a lone figure at the corral fence. From this point, he couldn't see who it was. "Early wedding guest?"

"It's a girl."

"Genius, brother." Caleb's voice held a grin. "That white dress give it away for you?"

Cody's pulse picked up speed. "Hann?" He tapped his boots in the sides of his horse and it easily complied into a canter.

The closer he got the more he could make out. She wore a lacy, mid-length dress, hiked it up, and then climbed to the middle rung of the fence. He smiled at the sight of her red cowgirl boots.

"'Bout time you got here, Cody McCall!"

The sight of her wide smile caused his heart to buck up to his throat as he came even with the fence line, tugging on the horse reins.

"I've been waiting most of my life for you." Her eyes shone with unshed tears. Holding onto the nearby post, she gingerly swung first one leg and then the other over the top rail. She sat there, capturing his gaze. "Well, cowboy, what are you going to do now?"

He nudged his horse to sidestep it to her. Leaning down,

he wrapped his left arm around her waist, meeting her stare. Wonder filled him at the soft, tender look. "Hang on to me, Hann."

When her trembling hands grabbed his shoulders, he lifted her and gently placed her across his lap.

"I'm here for you."

"I know, Cods. You've always been."

Her vulnerability touched a place deep inside him. "I won't let you down."

"You never have before."

"Trust me, Hann."

"I swear, I'll try my best." Her voice hitched.

But would trying be enough?

HANNAH PRESCOTT SHOOK. She leaned on Gramps' arm as they walked down the short, makeshift aisle. She drank in Cody. Tall and incredibly handsome, he never took his eyes from hers. His endearing face and steady calm plucked at her heartstrings.

Her leap of faith shocked her. This was supposed to be a fake engagement and lookee here, she was about to marry her best friend in front of all his family and their friends. They counted on Cody and Hannah to make this special union a saving grace for Gramps and the pride of the McCall Ranch. So much rested on their shoulders now.

It had been a last minute act of desperation. She didn't want to get kicked out of the boarding house. Even more, she didn't have the heart to disappoint Miss Peaches and Miss Clementine when it came to her character. They'd taken her in after her folks died. They'd nurtured her the best they knew how. They were more like her aunts than friends, even though their ways were old and outdated and she tried their patience many a time over the years.

The hope on their faces and the dreams in their eyes earned her all kinds of guilt over deceiving them. She didn't want to let them or Gramps down.

How could things have gotten out of hand so quickly?

A wedding! That meant marriage.

She gulped hard.

Gramps patted her hand and then halted at the end of the aisle. "Seems mighty funny for me to be giving away my new granddaughter to my old grandson."

That drew heartily laughter from the attendees.

The next few minutes went by in a heady daze for Hannah. She floated somewhere and only Cody's clasp on her hands kept her glued to the spot.

His brothers—his best men—stood behind him, supporting him.

She had her girlfriends, Sandy and Julie—all gussied up in new, soft pink dresses and perfectly styled hair—as her bridesmaids. They giggled more than once. And she had the sisters, both insisting on wearing dresses in shades of muted orange, like their names. They sighed and sniffled through-out the service.

Mr. Samuels sat tall and beamed.

The pastor spoke. She nodded when Cody did. She smiled when Cody smiled. A beat of silence followed.

And then Cody's brows drew together. He raised his hand and with his thumb he wiped a tear from her cheek. "Hann." His whispered word, filled with concern, yanked her to the moment and out of her foggy state.

Her heart hitched at the flash of hurt chasing across his green eyes. "Cods, I want to make you the happiest man." She choked back a cry.

And that was the problem; to make Cody happy she had to put aside her fears of disaster. It tore her in two.

"Just spend the rest of your life with me."

She cleared her throat. Gazing up in to his eyes, she knew what she had to do. "I, Hannah Prescott, take you, Cody McCall, for my best friend and forever husband…"

Hannah realized no matter what happened to them over the years to come that Cody and she were bound together for life. They shared a past and a present. Hopefully, they would work hard enough to secure their future.

CODY DANCED WITH his wife most of the night. They'd taken few breaks and only parted to pull someone else up to the makeshift dance floor with them.

Her steps came with ease, kicking up her boots, swinging around, and looking sexy as all get out. She laughed often and threw back the detested mandatory champagne for the toast. And she reached for him time and time again.

The band—Gunther, Jackson, and Harv—played all their favorites from old to new country and everything in between.

Family and friends cheered, his Gramps and brothers most of all. His cousins fended off Hannah's clingy girl-friends and shot him a withering look when Aunt Sissy came up from behind and gave them a group hug, crushing them together. *Subtle was not Aunt Sissy's style!*

The smoky scent of barbeque hung in the air from Uncle Jeb's famous brisket. The three-tiered white wedding cake with red roses stood ready to cut. The groom's cake, a replica of the McCall ranch—ordered by Hannah as a gift for him—waited on a side table nearby.

She gazed at him now, lingering and long, as she bolted back a root beer Conner handed her.

To everyone else, Hannah acted just like she always did.

It was easy to pretend everything was just like it always had been. But Hannah wasn't. He'd sensed it during the vows. He felt it and her unmistakable tremble as he slipped his grandmother's gold wedding ring on her finger and then sealed their promise with a sweet, slow kiss.

The hint of vulnerability widened and deepened. It was

more than nerves.

Where had *his* tough, strong-willed Hannah gone to?

"THE LIGHT?"

"Never mind, Cods."

He heard her struggle and then her boots, one after the other, hit the floor. A thrill shot through him. "Wow, you're not wasting any time, are you?"

"Why wait, right?" Her voice wobbled.

"How scared are you, anyway?" He reached out a hand, trying to find her in the darkness. The cabin's blue drapes were closed and he could barely make out any shapes even with the door still open.

"Was that you?" She twirled around and slammed into his chest. "Ouch! Oh, my head!"

Cody gripped her to him, steadying her. "Whoa, now!" The sound of movement froze him to the spot. A light clip clop went across the wooden floor. "What the hell?" He held her to him as he stepped back and searched for the light switch. When it found it, he flipped it on.

Bright light flooded the room. Cody blinked. Hannah turned in his arms and they found the culprit.

"Sweet Potato? Our very own peeping Tom." She giggled.

Relief raced through him. "Who put him in here?"

"That would be me!" Gramps shouted from the porch. Loud knocking came next as Gramps rapped on the open door and filled the space.

"Seriously?"

"Wait, you think I'd let him stay all alone at the big house? He'd gnaw on my favorite cowhide chair. Dang horse thinks he's a goat." He nudged Cody aside and nodded to Hannah. "I'll just take him on home now. Come on, little fella." He made a noise and the horse picked up his head and trotted on out the door, his hooves making light clattering sounds on the wood planks. "You two, have a very nice night."

Cody leaned on the door as he peered at the back of his grandfather waving the horse toward his house.

Hannah grabbed his hand and tugged him to her. "Come on, big fella."

He chuckled and shoved the door closed. "You are anxious, aren't you, Mrs. McCall?"

Pink bathed her cheeks. She planted her hands on her hips and raised an eyebrow. Her dress slipped and he had a glimpse of her bare shoulder. "And you're not?"

A curl of desire, low and deep, tugged to life. A hum in his blood buzzed. "Can you spell hell yes?"

She crooked a finger as she backed up a step and then another, dodging her hastily discarded red boots.

His smile grew. Cody plucked open the buttons on his white shirt. Her gaze wandered to where his hands were tugging the material out of his jeans now, exposing his skin to her. "I can't wait to kiss you all night long."

"That's all?" She gulped. Her stare swept over him and then found his.

Tiny thrills darted down his spine. "You're wearing way too many clothes, sweetheart. Can I help you with them?" It should have come out light and teasing. However, there was no mistaking the husky timber.

"You tell me. Can you?" She halted near the bedroom door, bumping against the frame.

Behind her, they'd cross over that threshold and step into another world. Her eyes glittered and her breaths came in short pants.

"I won't hurt you." The reassurance had nothing to do with making love to her.

"If I can't trust you of all people with *that* who can I trust, right?"

Stepping closer, he cupped her face in his hands. "No, Hann. It's not about that. It's about your heart." In slow degrees, he leaned in, watching her reaction. A flash of vulnerability sparked in her beautiful, hypnotic gaze.

"I so want you...us..." She reached up, clutching the flaps of his open shirt in her fingers. She didn't turn her cheek, didn't shove him away.

A vein of hope glimmered. "I'll catch you."

She closed her eyes and moaned softly. "Kiss me, you brave fool."

Her lips twitched the moment before he touched his to hers. *Soft. Sweet.* They moaned in unison. He delved in for more. Her hand slipped in between the fabric and rested on his bare chest. Cody sucked in a sharp breath at the searing touch. *She'd just branded him.*

"My head is spinning. My feet—they don't even feel like they're touching the floor."

"Concussion?" The grin in his voice made her chuckle.

"There's that protocol stuff you have to do, remember?"

How could he forget? He'd been banged up and broken down when tossed off a buckin' bronc many a time. Doctors swarmed him, checking out his condition. "Hmm...there is that. Safety first. Let me help you remove your clothes for your examination."

Hannah's breath caught. She skimmed her fingertips lower, leaving a trail of fire behind. Shifting, she backed into the bedroom, tugging him along. "Perfect idea, Mr. McCall. Where would you like to begin?"

His pulse hammered triple time. "The top of your head..." He slipped his fingers into her loose hairstyle and pulled out the pins. They dropped, pinging as they hit the wooden floor. Her hair, soft and silky, tickled his hands. "To the bottom—"

"My bottom?"

His laugh came out rough and husky. Lowering his head, he feathered her lush, delicious lips with delicate kisses. "Oh, I think I can arrange that prolonged inspection..."

Chapter Eighteen

I N THE EARLY hours before dawn, Hannah drifted in and out of sleep in the welcoming embrace of her new husband, curling into his side. Bare skin met hers. Warmth at the contact spread through her. She nestled her head on his shoulder, sighing in contentment. Cody's arm draped around her, resting his hand low on her hip.

Who would have thought it would be that great?

Cody chuckled. The gruff laugh tickled all her senses again.

"I said that out loud, didn't I?"

"Oh, yeah."

She jabbed him lightly with a fisted hand.

"Still feisty. Just the way I love you."

Hannah froze, tensing up.

"Easy, sweetheart."

His fingers brushed along her side, causing pin prickles of awareness to rush from her head to her toes.

"Sleep now. Talk later." His mumbled words did soothe her.

Don't make a big deal out of it.

"Exactly."

Her body, drained of all energy, gave in to the much-needed rest.

For the first time in years, she slept in total and utter peace.

He'll catch me when I fall...

"A SURPRISE? FOR me?" In the late morning sun, she eyed her new husband lazily leaning in the open window of her truck, still in awe that he was actually hers. His eyes, light green and shining, surveyed her. Goosebumps scattered along her skin.

"I know, you don't like surprises." He popped open the handle to the driver's side door.

Allowing him to assist her, she climbed down, highly aware of his touch and how he watched her every move. That spark of desire flared to life, or had it ever really died down? Either way, she still wanted him. She heard his mumbled groan.

Sounds like he still wants me, too. The tug of need pulsed again.

Putting some distance between them, Hannah walked around the bed of the truck and shrugged. "Where to, cowboy?"

"Turn. Some more. There."

In the far distance, she saw the metal chutes, corral, and a small, weathered outbuilding yards away.

"It needs more work. You can add on or do…whatever."

A lump formed in the back of her throat. "Cods?" She blinked back a sting of tears.

"For your bulls. This way you don't need to lease any property for them any longer." He scuffed his boot in the dirt. "You're a McCall now. You've always been a part of this ranch, so you bred, raise, and train them here. It's a brand new legacy for this land."

"I'll pay Gramps."

He jerked his head around to scowl at her. "Hell, no! You're family."

His fierce declaration shot through her like a lovesick cupid aiming it's arrow straight to her heart. *Family. Home.* "Suit yourself. But I *am* paying you back your loan." She held up a hand. "No bull, Cody. With the money I'm saving on renting from the sisters and now for the bulls, I can just give it to you." She smiled sweetly. "And you can do whatever you want with it, like settling up some of Gramps' bills."

Cody rubbed the back of his neck. "It's hard to refuse that offer."

"So don't." Hannah nudged him with her elbow. "Race you!" She took off running for the pens.

His bootsteps weren't far behind. Cody caught up, reaching out.

Hannah placed her hand in his and together they ran the

rest of the way together.

Could this really work? Could she finally have a real home instead of a broken one?

THERE WAS SOMETHING about walking in to the cabin and finding her there that made his chest swell and his heart jolt. Even after nearly two weeks of marriage and a few days apart for work he did with preparing the young guns for their rodeo stints it still did.

She—adorable in her red sundress and barefoot—puttered around the kitchen where delicious scents drifted to him.

"Hann, you're cooking?" He dropped his gear near the front door and slide off his dusty boots.

"Like I can't?" She threw him a grin over her shoulder.

Sexy. Sinful. Yep, that little devilish smile always got to him. His pulse hammered in his neck. "You make a mean baloney and cheese sandwich."

"Shame on you, Cody McCall, for calling *that* cooking."

Cody leaned a hip against a nearby counter, chuckling softly. He rubbed his jaw. "I've lost my charm, I see."

"Maybe your taste, too." She stopped stirring whatever was in the big pot, placed the wooden spoon down, and then turned to him.

Full on, she looked stunningly beautiful with her sweep

of hair hooked behind one cute ear, her brown eyes sparkling with mischief, and that slip of a dress that he was dying to remove.

"Think so?"

"Huh?" *What had she asked him?*

Hannah tsked him and shook her head as she drew closer. Reaching out, she skimmed a fingertip down his chest. "Why, Mr. McCall." She peeked up at him from under her lashes.

Something low and deep fluttered wildly. Cody bit back a moan.

"We're talking about taste here. Should I demonstrate?"

He raised his hands, giving up. "Be my guest."

"Now, that's a very cooperative husband."

The husky sound in her tone sent tiny thrills along his spine.

Standing on tippy toe, Hannah feathered light, delicate kisses along his lips.

Cody yearned for more. He settled his hands on her small waist and ever so slowly lifted her so now they were face to face.

She gasped, clinging to his shoulders. He wrapped an arm around her, cuddling her close.

"Better?"

Her murmur drowned out when she deepened the long, slow kiss. "Missed you," she whispered, nibbling at his lips.

"Can't be nearly as much as I missed you, Hann." Cody

delved in, prolonging the sensual feel of her body pressed against his and the taste of her luscious mouth. "We got time?"

The sudden noise at the door and the garbled male voices—dearly familiar—stopped Cody in his tracks. Gently, he eased Hannah down so her feet touched the floor again.

"That'll be a no, son." Gramps burst into the kitchen and headed to the stove. Sweet Potato followed, the dull clip clops of his hooves meeting the wood.

"Geez, get a fire extinguisher to put out the flames, will ya?" Connor's voice held a smile.

He emptied the two big, brown paper sacks he held. The beer bottles clinked together as he lined them up on the counter. Next, he drew out a bottle of wine.

"Family night at your house, remember, Cody?" Caleb patted him on the shoulder. "Forget, already? Miss Peaches and Miss Clementine would be sorely disappointed. That Mr. Samuels, too."

"And shocked to find you two like that, if you ask me." Gramps dipped the spoon in the pot and sipped from it. "Tasty." He took another one. "What is it?"

"Laundry." Hannah tried to keep her mouth from curving up.

Gramps sputtered, going pale.

Cody, Hannah, and his brothers chuckled.

"Almost had me there, Hannie." Pink brushed his cheeks. He straightened up, grabbed a beer, and then headed to the living area. "I'll just wait over there. But, by God, if it ain't edible I'll boot you all out and you can go live with the sisters."

Connor groaned. "Not that."

"Torture?" Caleb grinned, raising an eyebrow.

"Don't know how you did it all those years, Hannah." Connor shook his head, took two longnecks, and then went to join Gramps in the other room.

"Mind?" Caleb helped himself to a beer and pointed a thumb over his shoulder. "We'll just be over there. Oh, and we'll be able to hear everything you do or say."

"Just a friendly warning from our local sheriff, is that it, brother?"

"Don't you know it, Cody. I take my job seriously." He grinned and winked at them before leaving.

"Now I know why I didn't miss having brothers!" Hannah's voice rose.

"We heard that," Connor and Caleb called back.

"You were supposed to." But she giggled, shooting Cody a look. "You think we can find an old pillow case or something, boil it, and then serve it to all three of those jokesters?"

His chest swelled even more and he scooped her up in his arms, hugging her to him. Cody nuzzled her neck, inhaling her heady scent.

"They'll catch us again." But she didn't pull away. In fact, she wrapped her arms around his shoulders and melted into him.

He closed his eyes, thinking he'd found a slice of heaven. "Hann, thanks. For being mine."

HIS ENDEARING WORDS stayed with Hannah long after the sisters and Mr. Samuels arrived. The small cabin felt tinier but cozy with all their guests. Their hearty chatter and occasional laughter filled the air. They'd been welcome around the table with the makeshift extension to fit everyone.

"Chicken and dumplings!" Gramps rubbed his belly. "Hannah girl, my favorite."

"Grams taught me a few family recipes over the years." She blinked back a well of tears for their missing loved one. Nothing had felt the same without the dear woman, tough as nails and beloved by all. Right now, Hannah wished she was here, guiding her through these early stages of marriage and being a McCall bride.

"Mighty good." Gramps' praise meant the world to her. "You got promise."

"Glad to know." Hannah didn't take offense. She did have a long way to go. It didn't matter; she liked the gentle ribbing and all around sense of family.

"Great job, Hann." Cody dropped a light kiss on her temple.

"It's your turn next, Cods."

"Me?" He shook his head. "Oh no, no. I burn stuff. Like really bad."

Gramps coughed. "Wait, Juan and Rosa, too? They had to volunteer at the church tonight otherwise they'd be here."

"*Johnny* and *Rose*." His grandsons corrected him.

She pointed her spoon at each of them. "New rule. Everyone gets a turn. Including you, Gramps."

"Well, if you want Sweet Potato here to join in all you'll get are a few carrots and some hay."

Hannah burst out laughing. The others joined in.

"Pizza it is then!" Gramps eyes twinkled.

"Hear! Hear!" Mr. Samuels held up his wine glass and clinked it with the rest of theirs.

"To family night," the sisters said in unison, their cheeks glowing.

She gazed around the table, gulping hard at the dear faces. Keeping her distance hadn't worked over the years. They were a part of her just as much as she was a part of them. They were her ragtag family. *All hers.*

Gazing at Cody, long and lingering, her heart melted.

Cody wrapped an arm around her. "Everyone needs someone, Hann."

Including me, right? Or, maybe, especially me.

Chapter Nineteen

HANNAH SLAPPED THE metal trailer door shut and then locked it in place. "See if I defend you any more, you big bull."

He'd been especially difficult to maneuver today. Getting him separated from the three other bulls—all in different stages—she raised, down the chute, and then up into the trailer had taken over two hours of her precious morning. Bellyaching and backtracking seemed like a game to him.

Macho scraped his hooves and lifted his tail.

She jumped back. "Oh, no you don't!"

Nothing shot out of that end. Thankfully, it was only a warning—his way to show her his displeasure.

"You think you're funny?" She plucked off her work gloves and swiped the back of her hand along her forehead. "Behave, Macho. I got a lot riding on this one. No pun intended."

Checking on her other bulls, she made certain they had ample water and feed. She snapped every last latch into place, securing them, before climbing back in her truck.

The rough passage and dirt road took skill to navigate

around the pits and potholes, but, in time, Hannah headed down the backroads and to town. Trees and fields and cattle greeted her down the lane. She rolled down the window, breathing in the fresh, sharp country air.

"Might as well stop at the bank now since the diva—or is it, divo?—had a hissy fit. I'll never make it back in time to deposit that check."

And, dang, if she'd miss her second payment to Cody. His reluctance at accepting her money had been a challenge the first go round, so she took matters in her own hands this time.

"Do it first then tell him after. Done deal."

A smile played over her mouth whenever she thought of him.

They carved out time alone every few days when they weren't traveling—her for her bulls and him for training eager cowboys willing to learn from the one of the best on how to ride the buckin' broncs to get them in the rodeo ring and winning some cash.

Could she be more proud of him and who he'd become? Dedicated and devoted to his Gramps and the McCall ranch, he poured everything he had into saving it. When she could, she joined in the daily chores.

Caleb pitched in between shifts and Connor took on more duties around the property.

The least she could do was hand over her fair share on time. She knew Cody paid down Gramps' bills with what she gave him.

Country roads gave way to residential lanes which led to the outskirts of town. She slowed even more. At the stop light, she eyed the parking along Main Street and in front of the town square. Aware of the truck and long trailer, she reasoned she'd have to pull in to the bank parking area itself and take up the entire right lot.

Once there, Hannah peeked in on her bull. "No parties in there, right?"

He gave her a cursory glance.

"No good for the likes of you, is that it? Can't give me the time of day?" She grinned all the way into the bank.

The door whispered open at the touch of her foot on the welcome mat. "Ah, service." The quiet, elegant lobby caused her to check her heavy steps. She slowed and straightened her back.

"Hannah, how nice to see you." Mrs. Eggleston's sweet smile came from behind her large, neat desk. When she lost her husband a decade ago, she'd focused on her banking career, making it to the highly-regarded manager position. She sat in all her much-deserved glory as the first woman to do so ever at this bank. "How's Left doing?"

"Getting by." A nerve tugged at the side of her mouth when she tried to return the friendly greeting. It wasn't a secret that plenty of ladies had their sights on Left McCall now that he'd been widowed.

"You tell him I said hello and we miss seeing him come

in."

"Will do." Hannah scooted across the pink granite floor to the first open teller window. Looking up, she spotted her friend. "Sandy, hey you got the job!"

"Where have you been, girl?" She grinned back. "I know, with that hunky hubby of yours. I would, too, if I were you. Anyway, we miss you down at The Giddy Up. You and Cody need to stop by, you know, liven things up again."

"Is there a problem, Sandra?" Mrs. Eggleston entered the area behind the high counter and kept an eye on her new employee.

"No, ma'am." Hannah and Sandy answered in unison and then tried to hide their grins from her.

Digging out the paper from her front jeans pocket, Hannah slid the check along with the deposit slip across the sleek gray countertop. "You're such a help, Sandy." She spoke a little louder so her boss could hear.

"Deposit only?" She hit the keys on the computer, her gaze shifting as she read the screen.

As the bank manager moved along, Hannah let out a pent-up breath. "She always like that?"

"Only when my peeps come in. I guess she thinks I'll be friendly or something." Her mouth curved up at the corners.

"Wouldn't want you to do that now, would we?" Her friend smiled at the bite of sarcasm. "Maybe Cods and I can make it this Friday."

Her brows furrowed. "Hann, um. You know…" She

cleared her throat a few times. "This is a joint account, right?"

"Can't be. Cody and I haven't gotten around to merging accounts and everything." Put that on the growing list to add McCall to her name, go get her driver's license changed, put him down as a beneficiary, and all that other stuff she should have done already.

Sandy looked over her shoulder, waiting until Mrs. Eggleston exited the area, and then turned back to Hannah. The strain around her eyes stood out. "With his Gramps. Hardly...anything in it..." She swallowed hard.

A niggle of fear raced over her scalp and down her spine. It was worse than she thought. "Uh, the ranch..."

"I'm not supposed to."

"Please."

She tapped a few more keys. "Since there are multiple drafts from your new husband's direct deposits going to another account—the mortgage—I can just—" Her tiny gasp sliced through the air.

Hannah froze. "It's bad."

"Outstanding balance due." Her eyes were filled with concern and she glanced repeatedly at her boss sitting only a few yards away. "I can't say much else. I'll lose my job. I could already just for doing this much."

"How bad?"

Sandy gave a short, quick shake of her head and clamped her lips shut.

"If I guess, can you nod?"

Her friend's tight smile gave Hannah the go ahead. Her mind raced with numbers. A few hundred would not create that queasy look on Sandy's face. Obviously, her four figure check couldn't have put a dent in the amount, either. "Thousands?" The question, soft and filled with shock, spilled out of her.

The slight movement of her head spoke volumes.

"Ten?"

She gripped the edge of the counter, but raised her thumb.

Higher! "Twenty?"

She didn't change position.

"Thirty? Forty? Do I hear fifty?" With each growing number, her heart sank farther. "Sixty?" Her voice cracked.

The one brief nod told her everything she needed to know.

Hannah felt the blood drain from her face and maybe out of her body, too. Numb, didn't describe the half of it. She wanted to swear, loud and long. And then she wanted to break down in tears.

"I'm so sorry, Hannah. You can't say anything, promise."

She blinked hard several times. The stinging still came. Words failed her. This time she was the one to nod.

Leaving the bank, images floated in and out of her mind. Her boots hit the hard asphalt of the parking lot as she crossed the wide expanse, the hot sun reflecting off it. Her truck and trailer seemed so far away as her legs felt like lead with the awful news.

The McCall ranch hadn't fared well through the long Central Texas drought, only now on the borderline of going south again in a split second. Herds of cattle were lost and a small fortune along with it.

Helping the family load up sick cows and their calves had been gut wrenching, to say the least. They sold the healthy ones and what they could at a huge loss.

The more unfortunate cattle, well, Cody had refused to allow her to assist with the removal, sparing her that grue-some deed.

If that weren't bad enough for the ranch and the family then Grams got sick. She fought hard and long. Until she couldn't any longer.

And everyone—knocked down already—took an even bigger crushing blow to their hearts.

Losing the ranch might wring out the last of their will they had remaining—especially Gramps. Defeated, would he survive?

Tears spilled down her cheeks now.

Hannah couldn't let the McCall family lose anything so precious to them ever again.

But what could she possibly do to help?

THE BEAT OF the familiar tune pulsed through Cody. His cousin's band played the new hit on the small platform at The Giddy Up. "Thanks, Hann, for suggesting this." She matched his steps as they did the Texas two-step. Four other couples were dancing on the crowded floor, too.

"Pass up a chance to dance with you, cowboy?"

"Or toss back a cold one, right?"

She chuckled, but it held an underlying strangled tone.

"What's bugging you?"

Avoiding his stare, she shrugged. She moved with ease and that sexy sway of hers.

He almost got distracted, but refocused. He knew her too well to think this was nothing. The last few days she'd gone from quiet to clingy and then to jumpy. Sometimes living with her seemed like being with a different woman every hour. Some guys might like the shift. He didn't.

"Do I need to start guessing?" Cody didn't have a clue where to start.

"Oh, you know. The usual suspects."

The song ended and he directed her to the bar and away from their group of friends at the table. Sandy and Hannah had spent several minutes with their heads together, whispering when they'd first arrived over an hour ago. "Whiskey, Hann?"

"God, yes!"

"Desperate. Not good." He tapped the worn surface of the bar to get Buzz's attention and held up two fingers when he did.

The band struck up a lively one and nearly all the girls jumped up. Some of his friends did, too.

However, he watched his wife. "So, little lady, what's on your mind?"

She rolled her eyes. "You do not do good impressions, Cods, my dear."

He reached for his cowboy hat, took it off, and then gently planted it on her head, tilting it back so he could still see her beautiful brown eyes. "Better?"

"Much." She finally smiled.

Hannah brushed back his hair. She trailed her fingers down his cheek, along his jaw, stopping for a second at the small dimple in his chin, and then to the opening of his shirt, touching his skin.

A shiver went down his spine.

Leaning forward, she whispered, "Can I wear this again tonight? You know, in bed?"

Cody chuckled and a flare of desire raced through his veins. "Who am I to say no to you, bride? But can you take the boots off this time? You do get a little feisty and I think you left bruises with those heels of yours."

"As if!" She jabbed him with her fist. Her cheeks turned pink, though.

"I like when you blush." His voice dropped to a husky timber.

She licked her bottom lip.

The knot deep inside tightened.

Hannah peeked at him from under her lashes.

A bolt of fire whooshed to life. "I want you." He blurted it out. Cody never felt so out of control as he did when she was all soft and sexy and just being *his* Hannah.

Gasping, she sat up straighter.

"Here you go, folks." Buzz slammed the glasses down on the bar. "Earth to Cody and Hannah." He stretched out a hand, waving it between them.

"No offense, but get lost, Buzz."

"So that's how it is then…"

Cody waited two beats. "Is he gone yet?"

"Yep."

He shifted so now his arm rested on the bar and he drew within inches of her face. "You got a beef with me?"

Her frown came down hard and quick. "No. Why?"

"We're good, right?"

"Yes."

"So there's nothing stopping us from going up to the ridge and making love in the back of your truck, is there?"

Her gorgeous brown eyes lit from within. "Sweet talker."

"That's me." He pressed a gentle kiss to the corner of her mouth. "There's more where that came from."

"Kisses or the sweet talk?"

"Both."

"Multitalented. Hmm…I like." She cupped his face between her hands. "Stay still so I can kiss you back." Her lips twitched right before she touched his with hers.

It was hot and sweet and wet and long. Just the way he liked it.

They moaned in unison.

"Seriously? Can't you two give it a break?" Julie stood nearby. "Have some pity for the rest of us, will you?"

Cody groaned. Frustration tore at him. He slowly withdrew from Hannah's embrace. She looked as dazed as he felt.

"Has anyone ever told you, Julie, you're a wet blanket?"

"You don't have to be mean about it." Her voice broke.

At the same time, Hannah and he jerked to look at Julie. Her face crumbled into that ugly cry. A mixture of hiccups and sobs followed.

Dumbfounded, Cody watched as Hannah patted her friend's arm and gave him the raised eyebrow look. "What? I didn't mean it."

"Of course you didn't, Cods. There, there, Julie." She glanced around. "People are staring. I'll just take her to the ladies." Hannah tugged her friend away.

"And so it goes." The grin in Cody's words were undeniable.

Cody reached for the shot glass and tossed it back. It burned. He swung back the other one. *Nope, nothing's going to put out that burning fire he had for his wife. Not tonight. Maybe ever.*

HANNAH CLEARED OUT the small, two-stall bathroom. "Sorry, girls."

She let out a deep sigh. Her body hummed from Cody's kiss, never mind his hot, lingering looks. Hannah should have stopped herself from kissing Cody and just dragged him out of the bar at his suggestion. If she had, they'd be half way to the ridge by now.

Two of the younger local girls glanced at Julie while they stood frozen, putting on fresh eye shadow and lipstick, and then stared at her.

She shrugged. *Beats me.*

They hustled out. "Details. Later."

It wasn't like they wouldn't find out in this small town. And girls liked to talk.

Grabbing a nearby roll of bathroom tissue, she thrust it at Julie. "Sorry. One ply. Buzz still doesn't get the girl stuff. Okay, speak. Or forever hold your peace."

Now the blubbering began in earnest.

"What did I say?"

"He...I...we..."

"You're good with pronouns. But let's cut to the chase, shall we?" Maybe she could get this over with and be back to Cody in say five minutes.

Julie charged her, her eyes wild and unfocused. Hannah jumped back, banging her head and her back against the small divider between the stalls. "Ouch!"

"Thanks to you, I'm pregnant."

Shock reverberated through Hannah. "Me? Ah, sorry, that's medically impossible."

The range of anger and fear and shock chased over her pretty, delicate features.

Then she laughed until she cried. "I wanted to be loved. You and Cody, well, you've got something special." Looking at her with red-rimmed, teary eyes, Julie asked, "Why can't I have that, too?"

Hannah swallowed hard. All her life, she'd seen her mother like this—desperate and needy for a man, not any man, her own husband. It wasn't that he didn't love her mother at one time, maybe he still had in the end—especially since they were on their way to getting remarried—but it was never enough for him. *Her* mother *was never enough for him.*

"Does he know?" The question haunted her from days gone by; she'd asked her own mother that when she was only eight.

"No."

The same answer came back to her. "What are you going to do?"

"What would *you* do in my shoes?"

The weight of the world had dropped on her little shoulders then, suffocating her. The memory of it and the eerie similarity struck her to her core. She shook her head.

"Hannah, come on. My mama and daddy are going to disown me."

Same words. She flinched. Her mother's frightened face rushed back to Hannah. It hadn't taken long for her grandparents to discover the truth and throw them both out—turning their back on her mother for the rest of her life and Hannah's.

Her mother had groveled back to Hannah's father. The sad story repeated itself over and over again. *Marriage. One-night stand or affair. Yelling. Tears. Break up. Divorce. Make up. Rinse. Repeat.* Women were his vice. But that one awful time, the stress took its toll and the baby.

Even now, her heart ached for that precious little child. No wonder she didn't have much to do with kids after that; she could never get close, or attached—something was always stealing someone she loved away.

"You're my friend. I need your advice on what to do, Hann."

"Me? I raise bulls for a living. What do I know?" The edge of panic laced her last question.

People are not my thing! They hurt. They cry. They act all crazy when their hearts are involved.

"Plenty. You're so much stronger than me, Hannah. You'd have no problem taking on the world and maybe taking it over, too. But, not me. I've never worked a day in my life."

"So, get a job." Her words were short and to the point.

"That's so lame. What else do you have?"

"I'm the last person you should be asking." She searched

for a way out. If she gave her something, anything, maybe she could end this. "The baby comes first, now and always. What you want is secondary."

Julie yanked back, looking at her as if she'd grown two heads, like the calf old man Deyer's cow had ages ago. "Are you out of your mind?!"

She gulped hard. Straightening up, she smoothed down her blouse and brushed back her hair with a shaky hand. "You asked."

"I want a husband to go along with the baby."

Desperation clung to Julie just as it did her mother.

Jamming her hands on her hips, she glared. "All I want to know is how I can get Cody's cousin to marry me like you got Cody to marry you."

"One of the Laramie brothers?" For the life of her, Hannah couldn't figure out what cousin Julie knew *that* well or had known her *that* well. "Which one are we talking about?"

"Take your pick. There's three of them to choose from."

A glint in her eye sent a shiver down Hannah's spine, and not in a good way, either. Julie yearned for a cowboy and all that domesticated stuff tied up in a bow. "You don't know which one?"

She shrugged. "When a guy's drunk, he's putty in your hands. That's what mama said about daddy."

Warning bells went off. *Julie's mother, too?* "Julie, what are you doing?" Her head pounded and her eyes burned. *How could she do this to herself? And all over a man?!*

"And you weren't even knocked up. So, tell me, what's *your* secret in getting a guy to the altar?"

Somewhere far off the memory of her mother going to great lengths to keep her father rushed back to her. *Trap him? No, Mama, don't do it!* But she had. Just like Julie was trying to do now. *History repeats itself!*

Chapter Twenty

CODY HELD A shaking, shivering Hannah. She hadn't been the same since she'd talked with Julie earlier. She slept in fits and now thrashed around. "Easy, Hann. I got you."

In slow degrees, she crumbled, going slack in his arms. Her vacant eyes flickered open and then shut. He brushed back her damp hair and realized her nightshirt was soaked through.

Fear grabbed him by the throat. He knew about her bad dreams and restless nights for years. But this was the first time he'd witnessed her having a nightmare. He'd never known how horrible they were.

The echo of her cries waking him from a dead sleep still pierced his ears.

Shifting away, he slid out of the bed, keeping an eye on her labored breathing. Exhaustion claimed her. Padding barefoot into the adjoining bathroom, he went to the tub, dropped the lever in place and then twisted on the faucets, letting the warm water fill up the tub.

Cody came back for Hannah, finding her sitting and

rocking on the edge of the bed. "Hey, now. I'm here."

"Cods. It's so hard sometimes."

"What is?"

"Being strong. Tough."

He sucked in a sharp breath. "You don't have to be anymore. Not with me."

Shivers took over her body. "If I don't then I'll be like her."

"Who?"

"My mom." She choked. "Weak. Dependent."

"Hannah Banana? Weak? Never." He may be joking on the outside, but on the inside he shook down to his core. *God, it made so much sense now.* "Come on. Last one in the tub doesn't get the yellow, rubber duckie to play with."

Hannah stilled and then burst out laughing. "Is that what you're calling it nowadays, Cods?"

"Hey, it got you to laugh, didn't it?" He helped her up. She sagged against him. Cody lifted her easily and carried her to the bathroom. "Think we both can fit?"

"Me? Definitely. Not sure about that rubber duckie of yours."

He kissed her gently on the cheek. "My Hannah." His heart swelled with a well of love and pride.

"You sure you're not having regrets?"

"Never. You, my love, will never be boring."

She chuckled. It came out raw and scratchy. "Just neurotic."

"There is that."

Her heavy sigh rushed out.

Gingerly, he set her down on her feet. She swayed. "Hold on to me." He meant in all ways; however, he wasn't sure she could process that at the moment. He tugged her nightshirt up and over her head. "Hmm…"

"Now? I must look like a wreck and you want this?"

"Hell, yeah."

Hannah placed her hands on his bare chest and captured his stare. "You're one in a million, Cody McCall." There wasn't a hint of humor in her voice, just awe.

"Nice to know you think that of me." He swallowed hard.

It was a battle of wills to concentrate when she left a fiery imprint with her palms and her silky skin beneath his fingertips on her waist sent all sane thoughts scattering.

"You know the worst things about me, yet you still…"

"Love you." He finished the difficult words for her.

She bit her bottom lip. A fresh tear rolled down her cheek.

"That is nonnegotiable, Hann. Don't fight it. Don't be scared of it. It's good. It's real. And it's right."

A shaky breath rushed out of her.

"You're not her."

"Are you sure?"

"She couldn't find herself in all that was expected of her. She couldn't realize her own power."

"And strength."

"You got it." *But, did she?* Doubts seemed to linger in her big, expressive eyes. "Uh, looks like the water is at high tide. Rubber duckie time?"

Hannah giggled. The shadows faded. "You're good for me, Cods."

"You're just figuring that out now?"

Could she, though? Could she put the past behind her once and for all? They didn't stand a chance if she didn't.

HANNAH HAD SLEPT late. The woozy, drugged sensation dogged her still as she dragged her tired body out the door and the short walk through the gardens to Gramps' house.

Cody had checked on her before leaving a few hours ago.

She had too much time to replay her weak, trembling behavior. That vein of uncertainty grew. Clinging to Cody through the rest of the night, she wondered how she'd let it get that bad.

"You look down like that all the time and you'll miss what's going on up here." Gramps rose from the porch rocker. Sweet Potato reared up, stumbling to his feet.

Lifting her head, she shot him a weak smile. "Left McCall's little pearls of wisdom."

"That would be right." His gaze turned to concern. "Come on now, Rosa will be happy to see you."

"You mean Rose."

"She's Rosa to me." He guided her to the kitchen. "I told her I'd bring you by."

The pretty, brunette lady moved with efficiency and speed around the big room with the broom. "There's are Hannah. Hungry? I've got tortillas and I can throw together some sausage and eggs."

Her churning stomach tried to revolt at the thought of food. She placed a hand there. "I'm good. Thanks, though."

At the same time, Gramps and Rose's gaze dropped to her belly. Silence stretched.

That raw, exposed feeling surfaced. Hannah moved her hand away. "I hear I'm your driver."

"And Sweet Potato. Let me get his leash, though he usually won't let me put it on him." He marched down the hall and to his office.

She followed behind the miniature horse. It had been months since she'd been in the masculine room with leather and cowhide furniture and the massive ornate oak desk now piled with papers Gramps shuffled through.

"I swear it was on top ready to go."

"Here, let me help." Hannah dug in the right pile, trying to get things in order while Gramps moved to the left, making more of a mess. Her gaze fell on the pages—past due stamps. *Final notice!* She gulped hard.

"Any sign?"

"None." Her voice squeaked out as she found the buried

bank letter dated two weeks ago. He had less than a month to settle the entire past due amount or risk foreclosure. *That's what Rodney was talking abou, swooping in and grabbing up the ranch right out from under the McCalls!*

Nearly doubling over, she gripped the edge of the desk. *Time was running out! Why hadn't anyone realized it was this dire? Did Cody know how bad it really was? Did his brothers?*

"For the life of me, I can't figure out what I did with it." Gramps stooped down, checking under the desk.

With his back turned, Hannah folded the letter and shoved it in her back pocket. "What color is it again?"

"Brown. Leather."

"It blends in with the desk. Did you try the middle drawer yet?"

"Can't be." But he drew it out, ruffled through it, and then slammed it shut. "Nope." He straightened and his gaze landed on something. "Well, I'll be. If it were a snake it would have bit us, Hannie." Leaning across the wide desk, he plucked it from near the base of his bronze cowboy statue— the one Cody had won in his buckin' bronco days and given to his proud grandfather. "Got it." He shoved papers back in place and a map stuck out.

"The ranch?"

"Options." His grave voice held the weight of the world.

"What kind?"

"Never you mind."

"How bad, Gramps?"

His long, loud sigh bounced around the room. "If I can get a buyer for the west fifty acres…"

A lump stuck in her throat. "That's prime land." *Slicing and dicing the McCall Ranch? What would be next? Cody's beloved ridge?*

"Bring top dollar then. Problem is, I need interested parties with cold, hard cash."

"Isn't there another way?" *Anything, but this, please.*

"Running out of ideas and time." He patted her on the shoulder. "Don't you go worrying none about it. Something will turn up."

Soon, she hoped. These things couldn't wait until the last minute. Deals could fall through. A home could be lost.

A pool of dread hit her already jumpy stomach.

"YOU'RE THE DRIVER, so drive." Gramps gave her instructions over the next hour.

Sweet Potato swayed with the miles and bumped into her shoulder and then his. "Does he need a seat belt?" She rubbed the sore spot.

"Now that's a thought."

"Or maybe a cargo area. Or a pen."

"You sound like Cody."

A smile played around her mouth at that observation. "Now you have two of us."

"Now? Always been you and Cody since you were running around the ranch getting into trouble."

It seemed like it. *Only she'd loved him from afar.* Her mind slammed into that thought. *No! Yes!* She swallowed hard. As a friend, she could be close, yet still keep her feelings intact.

"Okay over there?"

"Why wouldn't I be?"

"You got real quiet all of a sudden." Gramps pointed to the dirt road on the left. "That'll be it."

She waited for the car to pass before she turned down the patch of worn out field with trees lining the way.

"Shame."

Hannah jerked her gaze to him and then back to the road. "What is?"

"Grams couldn't see you and Cody married. She had that knowing about you two. Cohorts. Friends."

A flash of memory sparked and Grams smile came with it. *Yeah, she sensed that their friendship could become more.* "Never said it to me."

"And scare you off?" He chuckled. "Hannie, you're the most skittish gal to be around whenever that topic came up. No, my Winnie realized that."

"See right through me?" She spotted the eight dusty trucks parked a few yards away—the old, rusty ranch truck being one of them—and the chutes and corral beyond.

"Good thing Cody didn't take it as bad as you would

have."

Pulling alongside the rest of the vehicles, Hannah shoved her truck into park and turned toward Gramps. "She told him?"

"Had a good sit down with him—and Caleb and Conner, one at a time—day before she passed. Wanted them happy. Wanted them to know—nope, not just know—wanted them to *feel* what love was like." His voice choked up.

"Like you and her." Wonder filled her.

"Yep. One of a kind."

HANNAH CLIMBED THE rails and then perched on the top one, watching the action while Gramps, standing nearby, talked shop with his two old cronies.

Cody instructed one of his students, checking his hand under the rigging as the gelding kicked and jerked in the chute.

In seconds, the cowboy gave the all clear and the large gate swung open, releasing the bronc. The student lifted his arm in the air and swayed with the jerking motions. He tilted to his right. One more kick from the rowdy horse and it sent him flying. He hit the hard ground with a thud and a groan.

"Good try." Cody clapped with the rest of them. "Next

up!" He had four more waiting for their turn.

So this was what Cody had been working on. She'd known it, but hadn't seen him teach. Even from this distance, she could take in the well of respect the others had for him. Around her, the men talked in awe at what Cody had accomplished with these young guns in only a few weeks.

A well of pride beamed bright in her. Cody had a way with people, always had. Likable, friendly, and patient, were only a few of the many compliments he'd gotten over the years. He'd give his time and money—if he had any—to anyone in need.

There wasn't a person on the circuit who disliked him. In fact, they invited him out for dinner, recap of the event, and many a nightcap, too.

Her Cody was known as the life of the party. She smiled at that. *Yeah, he was that. And so much more.*

Now, she watched as he took a turn, demonstrating the correct way to mount the horse in the chute, the way to wrap his hand…

Her breath caught. *Was he going for a ride himself?*

"Well, I'll be." Gramps climbed up on the bottom rung, beside her.

It had been nearly a year since she'd seen him like this, in his element. She sat up taller, gripping the rough wooden edges of the rail under her hands.

He went through with it. The gate opened and he was out. His body, like poetry in motion, moved back and forth with ease and grace. He sensed the horse's next step and went with it, not against it.

The whistle blew. Cody held on as the horse lowered his head and kicked up his back hooves, trying to upend him. The animal twisted to the left. Cody stayed strong. It went on for another agonizingly slow few seconds until Cody kicked loose and jumped down, dodging the horse's hind-quarters and then rushing to climb a nearby rail.

The small crowd cheered and some of the men whistled shrilly.

Cody's smile lit up his face. He threw his cowboy hat in the air and laughed. Hannah's heart tugged, hard and sharp.

God, she loved that man. She'd do anything, anything at all for him.

Now, she knew what her mother must have felt like.

Why hadn't she stopped herself?

Chapter Twenty-One

CODY SWEPT HANNAH up in a great, big hug and twirled her around. "Thanks for bringing Gramps. But I really wanted you to be here to see the guys' last day. Great, huh?"

"Yeah, you are."

He kissed her lightly on the cheek, laughing. "Not me. Them. You should have seen them weeks ago." Gingerly, he set her back on her feet, still holding her arm. "You okay?"

She nodded. "I am now."

But there was something not quite right. He couldn't put his finger on it.

"You're bringing Gramps back, right?"

"Sure. He's catching up with all his friends, so he'll be preoccupied while I pick up the gear. Hey, this is going to turn into a regular gig. This will bring in a steady income while I work the ranch this season. Not bad."

"Pretty damn good, if you ask me. You could always go back on the circuit."

He shook his head. "Bring in more bucks—literally and figuratively—but I can't be with Gramps. Or you."

Her smile seemed forced. She stepped closer and wrapped her arms around his shoulders. "Oh, Cody McCall. You would do that, give up your dream?"

"I've got other dreams, Hann." He felt her shiver. Cody whispered in her hair, "You and me."

"I…" She swallowed hard. "Love you, Cods." With a gentle peck on the check, she pulled away, trailing her hands down his arms and then finally letting go.

Cody caught the glimmer of tears shining in her eyes. *She'd wrestled with saying those incredible words to him.*

Watching her walk away, a heavy weight sat on his chest. *Why did it feel more like a goodbye than a see you later?*

THE TIRES HUMMED along the road as Hannah aimed her truck back to the ranch. Her mission set in her mind, she pressed her foot down on the pedal. With everything she had to do, she'd be cutting it close.

She made it in record time. Backing up the truck, she aligned it with the long trailer, jumped out and got to work hooking it up.

The bulls grazed in their pen. Birds cried overhead. And the sun beat down on her head. Still she worked in quiet desperation, knowing this was the only way.

Loading up her feisty bulls were another thing. They tugged her in the opposite direction, balking at her coaxing—gentle and otherwise.

"Come on, Macho. You need to move. Now!"

Her muscles burned in protest the more she forced the stubborn bull to comply. Grit and determination took hold.

"Just get in the damned trailer, Macho. This is the last time I'm asking."

Somehow it worked. He threw his head up and back and finally plodded his way forward. His hooves click-clacking against the metal.

It was another hour before she loaded up the rest, even though they were easier to deal with.

With the trailer shut and locked up tight, she took one last look at the empty bull pens. A well of sadness came over her. Hannah pushed down on the bubbling emotions coming to the surface. "No, don't you dare cry."

This is the answer. The only answer.

"YOU'RE JOKING, RIGHT?" Rodney lifted an eyebrow. He leaned forward. "You brought them with you?"

"They're all there." Hannah swallowed a sip of her water with lemon. She wished it were a whiskey. Sitting across from him at the steakhouse restaurant table, she'd rather be anywhere else than here. This place—her and Cody's place—had been bought by Rodney's father days ago, another feather in his cap.

"Wait, you barge in here, to my daddy's place and you want me to—"

"Buy my bulls." How many times did she have to repeat herself? *God, some men can be so dense.*

"You? Selling out?" He chuckled. "Never thought I'd see the day."

"My stock. Not my business." Hannah would be damned if she sold out her company or her name.

He shrugged his shoulders. "Same thing."

"Not to me. We have a deal or not?"

Rodney shook his head as he carefully placed his glass of soda back on the pristine white tablecloth. "It's true then. The McCalls are hurting for cash."

Hannah flinched inwardly, but didn't bat an eye.

"Just think, if you had married me you wouldn't be in this position. You'd have everything, including the contract for Macho to the big show."

Her heart jumped. She'd come so close to it. Doug Eastman and his partners were more than interested in Macho every time they saw him in the arena. But giving it up meant saving her beloved McCall ranch and allowing Cody to pursue his own dreams.

One dream for another.

Now she realized weakness wasn't her mother's problem. Love didn't make someone weak. It made them want to be loved in return. It made them *human*. And being a part of the human race was so damn stinking hard at times.

She shoved away her water. But she gave it one last shot. "We done here? I've got more miles to travel for the next buyer." She lied.

His jaw went slack and his face paled. "Nah. You can't."

"You were closer." She shrugged. "See you around."

"No, wait! How much for Macho?"

"All or nothing, Rodney. That's the deal. And it's a pretty good one at that."

"The others aren't ready."

"Maybe your daddy was right after all about you. If you think you can't do it…" She tilted her head and lifted her shoulder.

"I didn't say that. It's just it'll take time and money."

"You have both of those." She grit her teeth and gave him a tight smile. Rich kids like him had that in spades. Looking closer, she saw something flash across his eyes. She'd witnessed that fierce purpose when his father happened to be near. "Prove him wrong. Rodney."

A beat of silence dragged by. A slow grin spread. "Sixty two, right?"

"Make it sixty five and my name stays on them as breeder." Her throat closed over.

She might be selling her present, but she bargained for her future reputation in this business. Hannah could rebuild on that.

"Hmm…not sure about that…"

"Take it or leave it."

Now her heart pounded in her chest. Blood roared in her ears. The ranch rested on this one answer…

THE TOWN SQUARE'S clock inched to five o'clock. Hannah sweated out the last few yards, bumping into the bank parking lot and skidding to a halt. She shoved the gear in place and rushed to the glass door. It didn't automatically open this time.

Mrs. Eggleston stood with her set of keys in her hand on the other side. "We're closing in six minutes."

"So that means you're still open." Hannah pressed a hand on the glass, trying to part the doors. Thankfully, they gave.

"But…"

"I could be at the counter by now." She nearly ran across the lobby, her boots clopping against the pink granite floor. Hannah didn't stop until she found her friend.

Sandy jerked her gaze up from counting money. "Hannah?"

"Don't talk. Just listen." Out of breath, she dragged out the bank letter from her jeans back pocket and slide it to her. Next, she pulled out the cashier's check from her front pocket and slapped it down on the counter. "Pay off."

Her friend's eyes went round at the five figures and then checked the letter. "Hannah, how?"

"Never mind. Just do."

The sound of Sandy tapping the keyboard was like music to Hannah's ears. "I can pay off the loan and put the last few hundred in your account. Is that okay?"

She could only nod as she sucked in breath after breath. *Hyperventilating here!*

"The bank is closed." Mrs. Eggleston rattled her keys and came toward Hannah.

"Great customer service." Hannah shook her head, glanced at her friend, and then rolled her eyes.

"What could be so very important for you to barge in at the last minute?"

"Oh, I don't know, Mrs. Eggleston. Life. Family." *Love.*

Sandy stamped the documents and printed out receipts and then handed them over. "Buy you a drink, Hann? You know, after I count out my draw and close up. Say, fifteen minutes, I meet you at The Giddy Up?"

"That sounds good, Sandy."

What else did she have really?

Tomorrow, she'd have to pick herself back up and start all over again. She could catch up to the rodeo circuit, hire on as someone's hand for the duration, and scout out new bulls. It may take another seven years to get to where she'd been this morning.

Cody didn't deserve waiting on her or for her and the babies to come. The longer she took the more disappointed he'd be in her.

She couldn't bear seeing that in his eyes. *The hope dying. The huge let down. The life of the party slowly draining from him.*

Giving him up now seemed like her only choice.

Chapter Twenty-Two

"HOW MANY WHISKEYS does that make, Buzz?"
"You're at your limit."

Hannah groaned. *She'd only had two! What was up with him anyway?* Turning on the stool, she watched Sandy enter the bar. "Too late. I'm cut off."

"Already?" She shook her head as she hiked up her red, pencil skirt to her thighs and slid on a stool beside Hannah. "Buzz, can you give me a beer? Where is everyone? It's like a tomb in here. Sorry, she kept me longer. God, I think I need to quit my job."

"Why? What are you going to do?"

"Seems like anything else would be better than a stuffy old bank."

Buzz deposited the beer on the bar and nudged a tall glass Hannah's way.

"What's in it?" Hannah eyed the dark liquid with suspicion.

"It's called soda. I know, it's a foreign concept to your delicate taste buds. Do you need me to spell it for you?" He grinned.

"Funny, Buzz. Remind me why I still like you?"

"'Cause I'm your favorite bartender."

"Only when you give me whiskey." She smiled sweetly at him.

When he left them alone, Hannah watched Sandy guzzle the beer halfway down before she took a breath.

"That's bad."

"Hann, that money. It was your business, right?"

Something squeezed her chest. "My stock." She ran her fingers along the sweat on her glass. "I didn't give up my name. Not my business, either."

"I want to do that, too. Oh, not bulls. I'll never be as tough and strong as you. But horses, maybe. I'm good with them."

"If that's what you want, Sandy, go for it."

"What did Cody say?" Sandy winced; she must have seen her crushed look. "He doesn't know, does he? I mean, he'd never let you sell your bulls just for him and the ranch."

"No, Sandy. He hasn't found out…yet." She'd rather be long gone before that came to pass. Her heart clutched.

"Hey, no biggie, right? He'll come around."

"Trying to cheer me up?"

"You're never down—not like this. Come on, Hann, Cody can't stay mad at you forever."

"Wanna bet?" Her worst fears reared up.

She, Hannah Prescott McCall, destroyed every good thing in her life. Why should this be any different? *Just give me time and I'll decimate it, right? It was only a matter of time for her to do that to Cody.*

Instead of acting like her mom, besotted and fooled, now she'd pulled something her father would do. Keeping things from the ones she loved wasn't the answer, either. *Trust!* Damn it, it was something she'd come to measure everything else by—in her business dealings and the people she let in her life. It was a way to put up walls and keep them at arm's length, even Cody.

She swallowed hard. The one thing she valued most she'd gone and smashed that to smithereens with him. *How was he ever going to trust her again? Never mind that, how was he ever going to love her with his whole heart again?*

"Earth to Hannah. Hey, I need another one of these. Hold my place while I go to the ladies' room, okay?" She grabbed her tote bag and rushed away before Hannah could reply.

"Just great! I get to watch her drink."

Hannah drummed her fingers against the bar top. Minutes dragged. Buzz waved from the other end of the bar.

She could go tell Sandy she was leaving, but that meant having to enter the ladies' room again. Her throat closed. The last time she was there Julie had cornered her. *I wonder how that mess turned out.* Later, the nightmares came. "Nope, I'll pass on the bathroom meeting."

Picking up her glass, she took a tentative sip. She grimaced at the taste and the bubbles going up her nose.

"It grows on you!" Buzz yelled from his duties of wiping down the counter.

"Like hair, Buzz? Not everyone likes the results."

He chuckled.

Well at least one of them was having a decent time. She glanced at the clock. Fifteen minutes! Hannah groaned.

How much longer before she could escape?

"YOU SEEN HANNAH?" Cody entered the big house, finding Rose in the kitchen, stirring a pot on the stove.

"Not since earlier. You lost your wife already?" She grinned, wiping her hands on a towel.

"You're a comedian, Rose." He shook his head and pointed down the hall. "Gramps in his office."

"With the horse, of course."

"And you rhyme, too. A poet?"

"You're such a sweet talker, Cody. Can you teach my Johnny that?"

He chuckled, knowing his friend was not the type to compliment his wife. "I'll try."

"I know. Lost cause, right?"

Her deep sigh followed him out of the room. He heard Gramps' voice before he saw him.

"Come again? You sure that's right?"

Cody found Gramps standing behind his desk with the

phone receiver to his ear. Gramps looked up, catching his frown, and then waved him over.

"Now, hang on. Cody's right here. You can tell him what you just told me, young lady."

Scowling, he took the receiver Gramps thrust at him. "Who?"

"Never you mind the who, son. It's the, what the hell, you'll be scratching your head over soon."

He lifted it to his ear. "Cody, here."

"I don't have much time—"

Her whispered words crackled over the line. It had a strange echoing sound, too. Cody leaned a hip against the desk. "Start from the beginning."

"It's Hannah."

Cody stood up straight. "Is she all right?"

"Yes and no."

"You're not making sense. Is this Sandy?"

"Who else would it be, Cody? Seriously? Okay, Hannah did something today. She thinks you'll be ticked off, I mean like you'll never, ever forgive her for it. Remember when you had to chase after her when she spilled the beans to her mom about her dad's latest affair?"

He cursed.

"Yeah. That last one. Her mom was devastated. She told Hannah she hated her and never wanted to see her again."

"She never did." The next call came from Caleb—home on leave—about the wreck. Her parents didn't survive. His heart clutched. *The nightmares. The self-inflicted torture.*

"Hannah blamed herself. This one—the look, that downcast look—it's ten times worse right now. Like she's just lost her best friend in the entire world. You get my drift, don't you?"

"I'm on my way. Wait, where is she?"

"First, don't get mad, all right? She sold her bulls and paid off the delinquent mortgage on the ranch this afternoon."

A beat of shock rushed through him. He turned to his Gramps. "Hannah...saved the ranch!" His grandfather sank down into his chair, wiping the corner of his eyes.

"Cody, I can't swear for sure, but I think she's leaving. That look..."

Her words dropped like bullets in his ears. *Leaving me!* "Don't let her go."

Background noises came, a door squeaked open and then he heard her fierce whisper. "Don't think I can. She's antsy. She's pacing the dance floor now."

"The Giddy Up."

Sandy squealed. "She spotted me. Think of something. Quick." The line went dead.

Shaking, Cody dropped the phone back in its cradle as he stared at his grandfather. "Help me, Gramps. I need to win her back to me."

"Hand over that phone, son. I'm calling in the troops."

"YOU SURE THIS is going to work?" Cody gripped the steering wheel, his knuckles white.

"Don't know for certain." Gramps pointed a thumb over his shoulder. "Conner's bringing up the rear now and Caleb will meet us there."

He hit a pothole and the truck did a mini-fishtail.

"Whoa, now! Easy." He clutched Sweet Potato around the collar to keep him steady. "We got friends on the other side holding her in place."

Cody righted the truck and eased up slightly on the pedal.

"Wish your Grams was here. She'd know what to do."

"Me, too, Gramps. Me, too."

The miles flew by and his mind raced with what he'd find once he got to his Hannah.

How could she give up everything she loved? His heart stuttered in his chest. That was it, she was willing to cash in and leave town to save the love from turning to hatred. *Didn't she know he could never hate her?*

A bubble of panic rose to his throat, choking him. She didn't know that or else she wouldn't be scared witless.

How could he show her? How could he make her see love didn't die, not theirs?

"JUST A SIP, Sandy? That's your third and I'm on restriction over here." Hannah's head pounded. She shot Buzz the evil eye.

He laughed.

"I need this." Sandy stuck her finger in the foam and then tasted it.

"Seriously? Did you just do that? What a complete waste of a beer!" Hannah twirled around on the stool and hopped down. Her boots hit the floor with the dull thud. "That's it. I'm done here."

"No, no. You can't." Sandy's hand clamped down on her arm. "You owe me this at least for all I jeopardized for you the other day and again today."

"Guilt shaming me, Sand?"

"Did it work?"

The bar phone rang, startling her.

Buzz picked it up on the second ring. "The Giddy Up. You giddy on up here, you hear?"

Hannah groaned.

"That is so bad," Sandy agreed, still holding on. "Sit with me."

"It's for you, Hann," Buzz called out, plunking down the phone and the receiver on the bar.

"Me? Who knows I'm here, anyway?" She cut a look at Sandy.

She held up her hands. "Don't look at me." But she avoided Hannah's stare and played with her beer.

"Waste, I tell you." Hannah stepped back and reached for the phone. "This is Hannah."

"Oh, so glad I caught you, dear."

"Miss Peaches?" Her middle sank. Or was that the whiskey from earlier hitting rock bottom. She'd miss the sisters. "Everything all right?"

"We've found a…box of yours…yes, that's it. A new tenant coming soon…" She didn't make sense.

From the background, Miss Clementine called out, "You must come and get it. Right away."

"Yes, Clem, I'll let her know. Ah, Hannah, dear, could you please stop by and pick it up. You don't mind the short notice, do you?" Her voice dropped low. "You know how Clem can be at times. So very pushy."

"Don't I?" she muttered. But a smile tugged up the side of her mouth. *Good excuse to get out of here.* "I'll be right there, Miss Peaches."

The dial tone blared in her ear.

Hannah hung up and turned to Sandy. "I'm wanted by the sisters. Can't keep them waiting, right?"

"I'll go with you."

"No need."

"I insist, Hann."

They argued all the way from settling their bill with Buzz, out the door, and then to Hannah's truck. She threw up her hands. "Suit yourself."

"I thought you'd never ask."

She groaned, but shot Sandy a crooked smile.

In less than ten minutes, she navigated the familiar streets back to her old home. A little spot tugged inside her. She'd miss her hometown, miss the people, especially Cody. Now an ache burst behind her ribs.

There were several trucks and Caleb's police car in the driveway. Her heart jumped, recalling the night they'd sent out a search party for her. However, this time, the yard remained free of onlookers.

"Why are they doing this to me?" She blinked at the sight of the rusty old ranch truck. *Cody?*

"Go, silly." Sandy reached over and turned off the ignition, claiming the keys. They jangled as she held them up and away from Hannah. "No way out, friend."

Hannah swallowed hard as she climbed down from her truck. Wiping her damp hands along her jeans, she trudged to the sisters' front door while Sandy followed a yard or so behind her.

It opened silently. Caleb stood back and nodded for her to enter.

Her boots hit the wood floor with a muffled thud. "Am I in trouble, sheriff?" There had been plenty of times she'd had to face him in the past.

"Only if you turn around and walk out the door."

So many dear people waited for her. The sisters sniffled and pressed white hankies under their noses.

"Remember, dear. Don't look back with regrets."

Her throat closed over, recalling Miss Peaches lost love and her ongoing heartache. What was worse, loving and maybe getting hurt or not taking the chance and living with what-ifs for the rest of her life?

Mr. Samuels beamed. Connor rested a hand on his grandfather's shoulder. And Gramps' planted his hands on his hips.

Hannah gulped hard when she caught his direct stare. His eyes teared up.

"Well, little lady, you sure did pull a fast one on us, didn't you? Can't ever thank you enough for what you did saving the McCall ranch, but, I aim to try. Your mamma, daddy, and Grams would be so proud of you, just like I am."

She went to him and gave him a hug. "Not mad?"

He patted her on the back. "Don't rip his heart out, you hear?" He pulled away slightly and then stuck his thumb over his shoulder. "That way."

Even Sweet Potato nudged her leg as she gazed down the long hall to her old bedroom door.

Gulping, Hannah tread lightly, the walls feeling as if they closed in on her. Now, her ears thrummed with rushing blood and her heartbeat galloped in her chest.

At the big white door, she placed one hand on the solid wood and the other on the glass knob. With her breath hitched in her throat, she twisted the handle and eased open the door.

Cody whipped around to face her. His eyes were wide

and his face pale.

Hannah froze.

"Close the door, Hann."

"I'm scared, Cods."

"Me, too. Of losing you."

At his confession, she took a shivery breath and went to him, swinging the door closed behind her. It slid shut with a definite click in the nearly empty room.

She gazed at him, tall, lean, and strong. His beautiful, green eyes lingered on her face and then her lips. Warm tingles followed. That slight grin tugged up the corner of his mouth, showing off the adorable, little dimple in his chin.

How many times had she been lucky enough to see him look at her like this? *Not enough.*

He was strength.

"Funny, Hann, we've known each other all our lives and this is one of the few times we're speechless."

Cody was her light.

"Hell, I can't find the words. You did this for Gramps, my family, *our* family, for *me*." Awe filled his words.

He was her home.

"This is about the bond we have. The bond we've always had. It can never be broken, Hann."

Cody McCall was her best friend.

"I will live and die by that. Always."

And he was the love of her life.

CODY WATCHED THE tears well in Hannah's beautiful, brown eyes and silently fall to her cheeks. A hand clamped around his heart and squeezed.

Reaching out, he wiped the moisture away with his thumbs and then he cupped her face in his palms.

"I don't want to be like her. Hanging on when it had died long ago, or maybe it never was the real thing. It was the thing at the time. She just couldn't let it go, squeezing the life and breath out of it. Making them both miserable."

"That's not you. That's not who you are or what you stand for. Love shouldn't be wasted on someone who can't or won't return it. Love doesn't hurt, Hann. No...love heals. It soothes and fills up your chest with it and it spreads out until there's no more pain, only light."

"Talking from experience?"

"Yeah. You healed my broken pieces all along and I didn't even realize it until the thought of you leaving hit me. You make me a better me."

"I did that?" Wonder vibrated in her words.

"And so much more."

"You've always been there, Cody. When I stumbled and fell. You got me in and out of trouble. Through rough patches and smooth ones. To wallow with me or celebrate for me. Loaning me money to start my business. Even all those awkward girl stages, you were there."

"Oh, you had to bring up that." The weight on his chest lifted slightly.

Her laugh caught between a sob and a chuckle. "Feminine hygiene products and buying out a row of chocolate snacks and shots of whiskey."

"Not all bad, was it?"

She shook her head. Her trembling hands rose and settled on his chest. The warm imprint radiated through him, reaching so deep and erasing all the pain left there. "I can feel your heartbeat pick up speed."

Leaning down, he feathered kisses across her eyelids, tasting her salty tears. Her breath hitched when he trailed his lips downward. He halted, waiting for her to look at him.

Hannah lifted her damp, spiky eyelashes and gazed into his eyes.

This time, he sucked in his breath at the glowing light there.

"You believed in me, Cods. When no one else did, especially me."

"I still do, Hann. Now, you have to believe in *us*." He kissed her then, soft and sweet, until he ached for more.

"You once said that someday I was going to fall so far and so deep I won't know what hit me. And you hoped that it's with you."

Cody gulped hard. "I remember…"

"You were right. I love you, Cody."

"How long?"

"Forever."

"Promise?"

"Yes, my forever husband. I promise you that."

Cody wrapped his arms around her and lifted her, pressing her close. "I'll take it."

Hannah hugged him back, kissing him along his jaw and then his neck. "I can't leave you." Her voice broke. "You've always been in my heart and a part of my world. I'd be shattered without you."

Finally, she melted into him, accepting the truth.

"Thank God." Relief swept through him. He whispered in her hair, "I can't lose you. *Ever.*"

She sighed. "And who would have ever thought it all started by sneaking in a wind—" Hannah stopped abruptly, stilling.

"What?"

"Don't look now, but we have company."

He eased her back to the floor and then turned around, holding her to his side. In the wide, open window, crowded together, stood none other than the sisters, Mr. Samuels, Sandy, his brothers, and his Gramps—all grinning from ear-to-ear. Surely the horse was out there, too.

"Mighty warm in there. We stepped out for a breeze, is all." Gramps tilted his cowboy hat.

"Hell, Hann, we can't even sneak out the way we came in, anymore, can we?" Her laughter was music to his ears.

"I'm stuck with all of you, aren't I?"

"Don't you know it?" He scooped her up and twirled her around. "Love. Family. Forever with you, Hannah. My kind of life."

She sucked in sharp breath. "*Our* kind of life, Cods. At least for the next fifty years. Or more."

"I got you, Hann. Close to my heart. Always have. Always will."

The End

The McCall Brother Series

If you enjoyed *The Cowboy's Rebellious Bride*, you'll love the rest of the McCall Brother series!

Book 1: The Cowboy's Rebellious Bride

Book 2: The Cowboy's Reluctant Bride

Book 3: The Cowboy's Runaway Bride

Available now at your favorite online retailer!

About the Author

Bestselling author Laurie LeClair writes romantic comedy, contemporary romance, and contemporary women's fiction. Laurie's habit of daydreaming has gotten her into a few scrapes and launched her to take up her dream of writing. Finally, she can put all those stories in her head to rest as she brings them to life on the page.

Laurie considers herself a New Texan (New England born and raised and now living in Texas). She lives in Central Texas with her husband, Jim, who thankfully indulges her love of chocolate and storytelling.

Visit her website LaurieLeClair.com

Thank you for reading

The Cowboy's Rebellious Bride

If you enjoyed this book, you can find more from all our great authors at TulePublishing.com, or from your favorite online retailer.

Made in the USA
Las Vegas, NV
20 February 2021